REAL ESTATE PLANNING

HOW TO BUY A HOUSE

REAL ESTATE PLANNING

HOW TO BUY A HOUSE

Dr. Yogesh Sharma

PRABHAT PRAKASHAN

Published by
PRABHAT PRAKASHAN PVT. LTD.
4/19 Asaf Ali Road,
New Delhi-110 002 (INDIA)
e-mail: prabhatbooks@gmail.com

ISBN 978-93-90378-32-6
REAL ESTATE PLANNING
How to Buy a House
by Dr. Yogesh Sharma

Edition
2025

Price
₹ 400.00 (Rupees Four Hundred only)

Printed at
Narula Printers, Delhi

Author's Note

Buying a home is usually a decision of a lifetime. People spend their entire life savings to create a dream house where they can happily spend their lives with their loved ones.

Buying a house these days is not as easy as it sounds. Whether you intend to build your dream home from scratch by purchasing a plot of land or intend to move into a readymade flat, there are a lot of legalities that need to be looked into to ensure a hassle free purchase.

This book has been written as guide to creating your own home in the best possible way. It is a manual for those who are new on this path and for those who have already have walked on it before.

Updated with the latest techniques, tips and tricks related to purchasing your own home, the book will act as an advisor for people who are looking for advise and do not want to trust the wrong kind of people.

Your home is your own space, a universe where your family stays safe and sound. This book will help in enhancing your prospects in this endeavor.

This book also includes the concept of estate planning that is essential for everyone.

Acknowledgements

I am grateful to God almighty and my parents who have been a constant source of inspiration for me.

I am also grateful to my bank and its officials who provided me with opportunities to gain a deep understanding of the various aspects of banking and money management.

I am also grateful to all my friends, seniors and colleagues who have constantly inspired me to write this book.

Last but not the least, I would like to thank my readers who have constantly encouraged me with their love and appreciation.

Contents

1

Investment in Real Estate

Roti, Kapda aur Makan (Food, Clothing and Shelter)

Every human being has three basic needs. He needs to eat food to sustain his body, wear clothes to protect himself from elements of the weather such as heat, cold and rain. When the first two needs are fulfilled, every person starts longing for a house of his own—a place he can call home. Yes, there are rented houses available, but a rented accommodation does not provide that feeling of security or that sense of belongingness as your own house does. Today, owning a house is not as difficult a prospect as some decades ago but still the long list of issues that a prospective homeowner has to deal with tend to strike a chord of fear in most buyers. Moreover, one needs to be very careful in every step one takes in this direction because a small folly can mess up your finances and haunt you for years to come.

It is interesting to note that real estate is perhaps the single largest investment that most people make in their lifetimes, which makes it an essential, if not an integral part of every financial portfolio. Savings accumulated over the years are invested in a dream called 'my own house' and these savings can vanish in seconds if you do not know what you are doing. This dream causes people to spend nights toiling away at work and there are even times when people find that the money yielded by their hard work has been eaten up by the burgeoning inflation, which not only causes a dent in their plans but also leads to a lot of anguish.

Investing in real estate need not be a nightmare as considered by some. In fact, whether you are thinking of purchasing your own home or simply investing to get returns, real estate can be a very lucrative proposition.

This book will help you to understand real estate and its various aspects. It will also give you an insight into real estate business and the common mistakes that people commit when investing in this area. But first, let us talk about why do people need to purchase a property at all in the first place?

Purchasing a Property

When you start thinking about purchasing a house, the most common question that arises in mind is: What is the 'right time' to buy a house/flat/plot? My simple answer would be: The 'right time' is when you feel you are ready for the responsibility that goes hand-in-hand with the buying.

To make the right choice, it is important to consider your basic purpose of buying a house/ flat first. Why do you want a house? What motivates you to go for a particular one? Do you want to buy a house because you want to live in it, or are you looking for rental income? Or, are you simply buying it for long-term investment?

People purchase a property for two basic reasons

1. To use it as one's residence (residential purpose)
2. To use it as a source of investment.

The clearer you are in your mind about why you should buy a house, the more focused your search will be and the better will you be able to select one that meets your requirements.

For own Residential Purpose

As mentioned previously, every individual wants a home of his own where he and his family can stay in peace and harmony. To accomplish this aim, he either takes loans or uses his life-long savings.

Selection of Location: Different people choose different locations for their houses depending on their occupational and personal needs.

For Business Owner: People who have their own business should preferably purchase a house in the same city and as close as possible to the business premises or the head office.

For Salaried People: Generally, salaried people can be classified into three categories.

1. **State Government Employees:** Since most state government employees have transferable jobs, they should purchase a house either in their home town or in a city close to their hometown.
2. **Central Government Employees:** They should purchase a house in the state where they are permanently posted or somewhere close to their permanent residence.
3. **Private Sector Employees:** In the recent years, the increase in the pay scale and number of private jobs has led to an increase in the purchasing power amongst young professionals. Most of them are constantly switching jobs

across the country, so most of them may purchase property in different cities and states. Generally, they purchase the property for residential purpose but as soon as they get transferred, they sell the property at a higher price and move to a different city. However for the long run, it is advised that they should preferably purchase the property in a city of their choice or a city of their permanent residence.

For Investment Purpose

When you plan to purchase a property for reasons other than residential purpose (for rent or profit), it is termed as investment in real estate. The ever-increasing population and the increase in the purchasing power of the middle class have ensured that a long-term investment in real estate can provide high returns. Another reason for return is that the land cannot be cultured. Like equity, gold, mutual fund, real estate also belongs to a class of assets. But as an investment, real estate is like no other. It is simple to understand, tangible, and can greatly enhance the returns of your portfolio. The low volatility in real estate prices lends stability to the investment. The prices rise gradually over time, compared with other asset classes, which may see wide fluctuations. It also provides a steady stream of income through rentals, even during a lull in the economy. Even if you do not intend to live in the house, you can partly finance your mortgage payments and other expenses through the rental income. Besides, it also provides several tax benefits by allowing you to claim tax deduction on repayment of principal and interest on the housing loan, as well as repairs and maintenance. Most importantly, it provides the much needed diversification to your portfolio. But, keep in mind that there are different factors to consider when you buy real estate for investment or for personal use. Real estate is not a bad investment; however, it is important to take care that it should not be your only investment. It is dangerous when you invest only in real estate.

Where Should You Invest?

You may apply in various schemes of Development Authorities and Housing Boards. Every state has its own development authorities and housing board. These government bodies like DDA, HUDA, MAHADA, etc launch schemes from time to time and you may apply to invest in any of these. The only thing to remember is that in these schemes the allotment is through lottery system and chances are one may or may not get an allotment. You may also invest in the schemes launched by builders for residential township which may have flats/villa/plots.

There are Four Ways of Investment in properties

1. Purchasing a plot in new, upcoming or developing areas.
2. Booking flat(s) in a new multistory project by a builder.
3. Purchasing a ready-to-move-in-house/flat.
4. Investment in a commercial property.

1. **Purchasing a plot in new, upcoming and developing Areas:** Land cannot be grown or created. However, an investment in land is a good option since. The owner of a vacant plot enjoys an exemption from wealth tax. However, the exemption is subject to certain conditions. You can invest in developed plots in urban areas with a view to either construct a residential property for your own residence or to sell it at a profit. Whatever be the purpose, the investor must take into account certain important income tax and wealth-tax aspects.

   Where to buy? You should select an area near your city or village where state government or central government has an infrastructure project like ring road, railway flyover, airport, metro, underpasses, railway station, stadium, university, multi specialty hospital, SEZ, refinery, etc.

In these areas, when new projects come up, the activity of brokers/property dealers increases. This is known as the micro market of real estate. If property prices increase after your investment, it means your investment is right.If you belong to an urban area, you may choose a rural area which is to be developed by government in near future.

- ***Benefits:*** If an investor invests in a plot, there is no income tax on the deemed income from the plot, as long as it is not leased out or given on hire or rent. Thus an investor can take advantage of the increase in price and sell the land for a substantial profit later or show the same as a long term investment.

  However, keep in mind that in case you hold the land for more than three years, the entire income by way of long-term capital gain will become liable to income-tax at a concessional rate of 20%.

  Remember that form the Assessment Year 1999-2000, all individuals and HUF are eligible for complete exemption not only in respect of one residential house for their own use but also for a vacant land up to 500 sq. meters under the provisions of Section 5 (vi) of the Wealth Tax Act, 1957.

- ***Drawbacks:*** If an investor does not have sufficient money, he may resort to borrowing from a bank or from an organized agency or from a relative or a friend.

  In such a case, the point to be remembered is that interest on the funds borrowed for investment in the vacant plot of land is not allowable as a deduction as long as the plot of land remains vacant and is not let out on hire or lease. However, the benefit of interest on borrowed funds for investment in a vacant land can be shown as a deduction while calculating the taxable capital gain.

- ***Precautions:*** The land should not be under any dispute and the seller should be real owner of property. You must also keep in mind that the land should not be acquired by any local /government authorities in near future. There should not be any proposed project on the land such as railway track, highway or any such government project.

2. **Booking flat(s) in a new multi-storey project by a builder:** Always book a flat in the pre-launch period or at foundation stage. When you book a flat in a new project, you require less money because most of the projects adopt construction linked plans. Chances of getting good returns increase. If you take a bank loan, you have to pay the pre emi/per month interest only up to the construction of building. If price appreciates you may sell the flat for profit.

   If you are a new investor with limited finances, look for an under-construction property with a suitable payment plan and keep a horizon of 2-3 years for possession. But make sure you go for a reputed and reliable builder.

   - ***Drawbacks***

     1. The project may get delayed due to lack of funds or diversion of funds.
     2. Sometimes there are developments in a specific area due to government projects and new elected government withdraws from the projects and then the development in a particular area slows down. As a result, the new investors no longer take interest in the projects located in these areas, which makes it difficult for the builders to complete the projects.
     3. Delayed project due to reasons like strike, higher labor cost, etc.

4. The builder changes the proposed dimensions of the carpet area without informing.
5. Abundance of property in that particular area at competitive rates.
6. The prices of flats/apartments appreciate less in comparison to plots, houses and commercial property. However, loans are easily available for such flats.

3. **Purchasing a ready-to-move-in- house:** If you have the required finances, ready-to-move-in is the ideal option for you as an end-user. Purchasing ready-to-move-in house means that unlike an under-construction home, you don't need to wait to move in to your new home. Moreover, you only get what you see, since the house is ready, the area is developed and there are people living there.

This property would be significantly more expensive than at the foundation stage but you as a buyer are protected against time and cost over-runs. Since the project structure is ready and possession will take place shortly, you are assured of the time frame within which you will be able to occupy the house. It also saves you from paying the EMI during the period when the house is under construction. If you are buying a house for future use or even to serve as a means to supplement your income through regular rental returns, ready-to-move-in property brings immediate rental income which also helps repay the loan availed to buy the property.

❖ ***Drawbacks:*** A ready-to-move-in house is obviously a costlier option as compared to an under-construction property, which implies that the installments will be higher. Moreover, unlike an under-construction property, the scope of price increase is not as high, which means that you may not be able to earn a lot of profit by selling the property at a later date.

- **New or Resale?:** The biggest benefit of buying in the resale market is that the construction is almost complete. This can be a big relief at a time when most projects are getting delayed. Also, not all resale properties in the market are old ones; most have probably never been lived in. In some cases, such as properties that were lapped up by investors at the pre-launch stage, the price may be lower than the builder's tag. However, in the resale market the down payment maybe higher. The seller may also ask for a portion of the price to be paid in cash, which means that you will be able to take a smaller home loan because seller will draw an agreement to sell at a lesser amount than the stated cost. The home work and paperwork required in case of a resale project may also be more.

Becoming a house owner means not having to deal with pushy landlords, poor maintenance and annual rental hikes. Plus, there's the feeling of having fulfilled one of life's most important financial goals.

While the satisfaction of owning your own house is indeed a great motivator, when it comes to the financials, the rental income is 3 to 5 % of annual value of property and also attracts income tax on it. Moreover, these days, it is difficult to find good tenants. It is also not certain that house will be on rent for the whole year or not.

In effect, the rental income may just be a small fraction of the entire cost of the house. For example, if the house cost is ₹40 lakh then rental income per annum will be ₹1.20 lakh to ₹2 lakh.

Whether you rent it out or live in it, owning house comes with its own worries: you get tied to a location and moving becomes difficult; you need to pay an EMI for a number of years; and selling the house is not easy in case you need cash at short notice. For some people, the above mentioned reasons might just be why they opt for renting a house rather than buying one even though it may feel like throwing the money down a sinkhole.

4. **Investment in commercial property:** It is a better option to invest in office showrooms, shops, etc. We can earn income from rent as well as from price appreciation. However, despite all the benefits that result from investing in a commercial property, the investments are mostly made by rich and institutional investors.

   There are four ways of investing in a commercial property:

   i. Direct purchase from builder.

   ii. To purchase shares of real estate companies.

   iii. Real estate investment trust (REIT).

   iv. To invest in mutual funds which invest in commercial real estate companies.

   You should select a commercial property which can be let out after purchase. Select n commercially active area or which has the prospect becoming commercially active in the near future. When investor invests in small units, it is more profitable if it is in prime location. At a prime location, it is easy to rent out the property. The investor may also use it for his own business. Doctors, lawyers, CA and businessmen use these commercial places to set up their own office or practice. Before investing, the investors need to ascertain that factors such as the economical conditions, job market, population growth and other conditions are favorable.

   In case of commercial properties, you should purchase a property which is ready or will be ready within 5 to 6 months. Now-a-days it is presumed that commercial real estate is over supplied. So investing in commercial real estate may be a risky proposition.

Just like putting all the eggs in one basket is not a good choice, investing only in real estate is a risky proposition. It is important to invest in different sectors as it helps us to deal with market fluctuations. It is important to ensure that you have enough diversification and liquidity in your portfolio before investing in real estate.

Benefits

The biggest advantage of investing in office spaces is the higher rental return as compared to a residential property, which is a paltry 1.5-2.5% as compared to a rental return of 7-8%. If you factor in the 30% standard deduction, your return is even higher. The rental income increases by 5-7% annually, and the property's value also appreciates over the years, though the rate of appreciation is not as high as for a residential property. In these troubled times, when the fear of unemployment looms large, it is imperative to have alternative sources of income. Another benefit is that if you are bitten by the entrepreneurial bug, an office property can help make a smooth transition. If you decide to start a business or consultancy when you are in your 40s or 50s, the switch will be easier if you can avoid the burden of monthly rentals.

Disadvantages & Risks

1. The foremost risk of investing in an office space is that it may remain vacant due to the lack of tenants. Meanwhile, you will have to continue spending on maintenance. The rental income from office space is tied to the economic cycle. If a building was prepared for IT clients, and this particular industry is caught in a slow-down, you may find occupiers

hard to come by. You may also have to compromise on rent. Besides, raising the rent when the lease is up for renewal may be difficult.

2. Most residential properties are purchased using a bank loan, but if you want to buy an office property, you may find it tough to persuade a bank to grant you one. Banks don't lend unless the property is tenanted or you have another property that you can mortgage.

Remember to Invest According to your Risk Appetite

You can invest in an office property at any of the following stages:

- When the building is under construction
- When construction is over but the property is vacant
- When the building is ready and occupied.

The advantage of buying a property that is under construction is that the purchase price is low. Investing at this stage could fetch you the highest price appreciation. However, the risks are also the highest at this stage. The builder may not complete the project on time, hence your returns may start coming in from a date later than you anticipated. There may also be a question mark on the quality of the product that will be delivered. To mitigate these risks, opt for a reputed developer.

If you invest when the building is ready but vacant, you run the risk of delay in finding a tenant. When you do find a tenant, the rent he is willing to pay may be lower than your expectations. If you invest when the building is occupied, your risks are the lowest, but you are likely to enjoy minimal capital appreciation.

Investors with the highest risk appetite should invest at the first stage, and those with the lowest, at the third. If you are investing for rental yield, do so in an occupied property, but if you are investing for capital gain, go for a Greenfield project. Conservative investors should also opt for an occupied property.

Investigate Before Investing

As with all real estate transactions, give priority to location. Look at the key economic drivers in the location. Also ensure that the basic amenities such as water and electricity supply especially when your building is ready. If there are issues with the basic amenities, it will affect both your ability to find tenants and the rent you earn.

While investing in suburbs, avoid remote locations that lack good connectivity to a highway. The surrounding infrastructure, such as internal roads in the locality, also must be in good condition.

Next, consider the construction quality of the building. There may be only a couple of reputed developers developing office property in the area of your choice. The range of choices will depend on the location.

Make enquiries in the locality about the rental return you are likely to earn from the building. Find out about the popularity of the area and the influx of tenants in the area, i.e. if the tenant leaves how long it will take to find another. In the case of an already occupied property, make sure that the tenant has a business that is profitable and growing. This will help avoid the risk of the property falling vacant at an early stage. Also go through the lease agreement. If required, have it vetted by a lawyer. At the very least, it should have a lock-in period.

Drawbacks of Real Estate Investment

- ***Liquidity:*** The main drawback/risk of real estate investment is that when you require money urgently and you want to sell your property, it takes time. In this way, it is an illiquid asset. So in case of emergency, you cannot depend on your real estate investment and even if you do, chances are that you may have to sell it at a low price.

- ***Scams and Frauds:*** Like any investment, one needs to invest in real estate with care. There are fraudsters who may create false documents of property and may sell it to many buyers. This is particularly common in case of an open plot since it has no particular identification of possession. Many fraudsters take money and vanish overnight. At times, your property, especially if it is in another city may be illegally occupied by unauthorized people who pose either as property owners or tenants. Sometimes, if you are not careful, some scammers may sell you properties which have a court stay. There have been cases where people have signed and sold their property only to discover that the payment cheque has bounced and they have only received part of the payment.
- ***Delayed projects:*** Sometimes the builder may not complete the project in the given deadline. This may result in losses to the buyer which may include the additional interest of the house loan and the additional rent payment.
- ***More amounts are required to invest:*** It is definitely more expensive than other investments such as bonds or gold.
- ***Property prices may decrease:*** It is not necessary that long term returns may be good. Generally, like shares, property gives good returns in a period of about 25 to 30 years. Real estate, like other asset classes, goes through periods of ups and downs. The only difference is that it is not as volatile as, say, stocks or gold. Property prices in some markets have been stagnant for the past 1-2 years. In fact, some areas have actually witnessed a fall in prices.

Also, remember that buying a house in a far-flung area may be cheap, but will come with other costs, including long commutes to office, children's school, weekend shopping, social visits, etc. As a tenant, you should always choose a well-connected location from where it is easier to commute to office and other places.

How Much Appreciation can be Expected in Real Estate

In real estate investment there is no rule of the thumb regarding return and property markets go through positive and negative cycles. However, normally values do not drop. Sometimes they simply don't rise for a couple of years. Normally when you enter at lower prices early in the development cycle or into more affordable properties in the mid-level and affordable housing segments, they record healthy appreciation in capital values in the short term from a low base. High-value/premium properties have lower rates of appreciation. You spend more to buy a big premium house, but remember that since the ticket size is large, you may find it that much more difficult to find a buyer when you are looking at an exit option.

The best investors are those who see a rising price and sell when they have reached their realistic benchmarks of appreciation. If you monitor your investments regularly, you would be able to assess when to exit. It is a good idea to check out the historical property values in your neighborhood. Assessing rates and trends over a period of time will allow you to understand how the property values have behaved in the past and predict have they will behave given similar conditions.

❑

2

Real Estate Investment Trust (REIT)

In India, real estate investment trust is a new emerging asset class, capable of generating a stream of regular income for investors. This has particularly become popular because in this case, the investors can earn profit from this sector without a direct investment.

A REIT is a company that mainly owns, and operates income producing real estate such as showrooms, shopping centers, offices, hotels and warehouses.

Globally, REITs are now present across 40 countries, manage over $ 2 trillion in assets and account for a fifth of all property market transactions. It provides portfolio diversification plus a strong and reliable dividend income. In developed countries where REITs have existed for decades, they have demonstrated excellent long- term risk-adjusted returns, as well as the liquidity and transparency of public money. In India, REIT will create a practical way for all investors to invest in large-scale, income producing, professionally managed companies that own commercial real estate.

Securities and Exchange Board of India (SEBI) is the regulator for this asset class, so the investors need not worry about the authenticity and return on their investment. According to the SEBI, a REIT is set up as a trust and has parties such as trustee (registered with SEBI), sponsor, manager and principal valuer with specific responsibilities. After the registration, REIT would raise funds through an initial offer from investors and get listed. The minimum issue size of the initial offer has been specified at ₹250 crore and the regulator has specified that the size of assets under the REITs should not be less than ₹500 crore.

IPO of India's first RIET (Embassy Office Parks REIT) was launched on 18th March 2019. Shares of Indian REIT started trading from 1st April 2019 in Bombay Stock Exchange.

REIT invests in commercial real estate assets, either directly or through special purpose vehicles (SPV). The introductory schemes will include close-ended real estate investment schemes like close ended mutual fund that will invest in property with the aim of providing returns to unit holders. The returns will be derived mainly from rental income or capital gains from real estate.

For REIT's there is a mandate that out of all Net Profit (PAT), at least 90% should be paid out as dividends to its shareholders. It means, not more than 10% of PAT(Profit After Tax) can be kept as retained earnings by REIT's in India.

REITs are similar to mutual funds and shares and provide income to its investors in two ways.

- ***Dividend:*** RIETs pay dividends to its shareholders.
- ***Capital Appreciation:*** As REITs stocks are listed in BSE and NSE, price appreciation of its shares will also make money.

It can raise funds from both domestic and foreign investors but initially the units of REITs are offered only to HNIs/ institutions and therefore, the minimum subscription size has been kept at ₹50000 only.

Investors in the age-group of 45-50, seeking a steady inflation-hedged, tax friendly income stream and does not involve very large amounts can consider investing in REITs, as these instruments are a good options for post-retirement savings.

Everyone can benefit from owning at least some real estate as part of their investment portfolio. REITs are the doors which open for those who do not own land or any other form of real estate.

Since, it is regulated by SEBI, we can be certain that the product is extremely safe. Nevertheless, we need to understand aspects like returns, volatility and benchmark from an investment point of view. One indicator is that unlike ownership in land or a residential or commercial property, REITs will involve diverse holdings to make sure they pay out regular dividends from completed, income-generating properties as this ensures a minimum return and thus reduces the risks to investors. However, this does not ensure that the NAV will not be volatile.

While the REIT itself attracts no tax, the entities or firms or companies from which it collects rents will have to shell out taxes. Likewise, investors will have to pay taxes on the dividends as well as capital gains they make on their REIT investments. Effectively REITs will compete with conventional real estate and at the same time compete with other ultra-safe investments on returns such as PPF and debt funds.

REIT favors the investor on liquidity front unlike the real estate investments in residential or commercial properties where liquidity could pose problems. If you are in early stage of service or business and can do only make small investments in real estate, this could be a start. Once you have accumulated sufficient funds, the proceeds can be used to purchase a real estate of your choice. This process is similar to making investments in gold funds and ETFs which help in accumulating gold for consumption (for example in case of family weddings) in the long term.

❑

3

Real Estate Investment for Children and Minors

Normally, in India when a child is born, some relatives may gift the child money or gold besides the general gifts. As a result, in many cases parents get a handsome amount of cash in hand.

Generally, most of the people open a bank account in the name of child (under guardianship) and make a fixed deposit..

Some grandparents gift a fixed deposit to their grandchild every year. I worked for eight years in the banking sector and I met many grandparents and some parents who a like to gift a fixed deposit to their child every year. Obviously, there is a sentimental value attached to the gift which also helps in creating resources and investments for the child's future.

Most parents know that prices and expenses tend to increase with time. Education is costly-particularly higher education and so is marriage. Generally, when the child turns 18, additional funds are required for education and after some years, marriage. Many parents tend to opt for insurance policies. The insurance agent or consultant suggests that the parents sign up for a child plan, where they give a monthly or yearly premium which will ensure that the parents get a good lump-sum amount when the child turns 18, which will help them to take care of education and marriage. They also state that in the event of death of either parent, the sum assured will be provided to the child and the remaining policy premiums will be paid by the insurance company and the child will benefit from the returns on the investment after 18 years of age. However, insurance is an instrument to insure against any unforeseen event and not generally used for long-term investments. Instead of investing in the child's name, it is better to take a life insurance in your own name, which will help you to take care of your liabilities.

As per my extensive experience in banking and real estate, I suggest that in case you do want to invest for your child's future, you should purchase a plot (a piece of bare land with or without boundary wall without any construction) in the name of your minor child. This is one of the best investments available in the world. The plot may be residential or agricultural. Your investment may vary from ₹1 lakh to ₹10 lakh according to your capacity to invest.

As we have already discussed, as per section 64 of income tax, since the plot will not generate any income hence it will not affect your tax liability until the child is minor.

While purchasing a plot, ensure that you choose the right location. You should select an undeveloped area which has prospects of being developed in the future. This will ensure your investment will grow in value with time and ensure adequate returns for your child in the future.

❑

4

Should you invest in your Wife's Name?

One day my friend Mr. Atul came to my office and told me that he wanted a home loan since he had decided to purchase a new flat. During our conversation, he showed me the sale agreement. It was in the name of his wife, Mrs. Deepika. He further told me that he had already purchased a house in his name and since Deepika was employed, so she would be able avail the tax benefit Thus like Atul, many prudent tax payers and investors invest in the name of ladies.

Investing in the name of the ladies has certain benefits which include.

1. Several states charge lower stamp duty on properties if it is purchased by women. For example, In Rajasthan property purchased by ladies attracts 1 % less stamp duty as compared to the investments made by men.
2. If a woman purchases a house and avails home loan she may take benefit of Section 80C and 24 of Income Tax.
3. Buying a property in a lady's name and letting it out on rent may also attract additional tax exemption.
4. Some banks offer lower rate of interest for women.

It helps women to enhance their self esteem and sense of security. Let us look at section 64 of income tax which in reference to clubbing of income tax. It states that income derived from the money gifted to a wife will be treated as the income of her husband. It will be clubbed with his income for the year and taxed accordingly. Hence, it is clear that a married woman should not be gifted any property by her husband, father-in-law or mother-in-law to avoid any clubbing of income.

For instance, if you buy a house in your wife's name but she has not monetarily contributed in the purchase, then the rental income from that house would be treated as your income and taxed at the applicable rate. So when you want to invest in your wife's name, give her loan on a reasonable rate of interest to avoid conditions stated in e section 64. Hence, though a married lady cannot receive a gift from her husband or in-laws, she can definitely get a loan from them. If this step is taken, there will be no that hassles in buying a property in the name of your spouse.

❑

5

Role of Hindu Undivided Family (HUF) in Real Estate Planning

Every individual is interested in saving his tax and this is only possible by taking advantage of the various provisions contained in the Income Tax Law. There is a difference between tax evasion (by resorting to illegal activities such as money laundering or black money) and saving tax by following certain legal practices.

A prudent investor can save income tax using a legally recognized method i.e. formation of a separate tax entity which is officially recognized and approved under the Income-Tax Law and is known as HUF (Hindu Undivided Family).

We cannot create HUF but can arrange capital for it. Initially HUF is an empty balloon that no one has yet blown air into. A balloon can rightfully be called a "balloon" only when it swells up with air inside it. In the same manner an HUF is dormant without funds. To form an HUF, you have to be married.

Step by Step Formation of a HUF

- **Deed:** Though it is not mandatory to have a deed for the formation of an HUF, it is advisable to execute one from a legal and taxation perspective. It should contain the details of the karta, members of the HUF (coparceners), other family members and the corpus as well as the business of the HUF.
- **Members:** An HUF is automatically constituted after marriage. Suppose your father is a karta of HUF and you are coparcener. Now after your marriage a new HUF can be formed by the partition of an existing HUF into multiple units. A suitable name needs to be given to the HUF, suppose your name is Sunil Kumar then you may name your HUF as Sunil Kumar HUF.
- **PAN:** You as a karta of an HUF should apply for separate PAN and quote the PAN while making investments and carrying out business activities or purchasing properties in the name of HUF.
- **Bank Account:** After obtaining a PAN card you should open a bank account first in the name of HUF so that you can do transaction using cheques and may deposit the generated income in bank account.

Formation of Capital of a HUF

An important requisite for the constitution of an HUF is its corpus or capital. This capital is separate from the assets owned by its members. Your father/mother/in-laws may gift money to your newly-created HUF, clearly specifying in the Gift Deed that the gift is to your smaller HUF and not to yourself. The property received by way of a Will in favor of the HUF can become the corpus. Transfer money by gifts to HUF capital keeping in view the clubbing provisions and tax on gifts under income tax act.

Remember that you should not gift anything to your own HUF otherwise there will be no benefit of formation of HUF. Friends and other relatives can give gifts but only up to ₹50000 (Section 56). A way-out is to receive gifts from members of bigger HUFs, who are though your relatives but are not included as members of your smaller HUF.

After the HUF has a nucleus of its own and gets going, care has to be taken to keep the HUF's affairs completely distinct from the individual member's affairs. Maintain separate bank account for your HUF. The members of the HUF carry on their individual businesses, as they normally do.

Can A Daughter be a Coparcener in an HUF?

Yes!

On 9th September 2005, the Hindu Succession Act, 1956 was amended to provide that a daughter too could be a coparcener i.e. joint heir, like her brother to the joint family's assets and she too could enforce the partition of the family property to claim her individual share.

She continues to be the coparcener in her father's HUF even after she gets married and forms another HUF with her husband. According to latest changes in the law, which state that the female members of an HUF continue to be its members even after marriage. Thus if you have a daughter, she would continue to be a member of your Hindu Undivided Family even after her marriage.

A coparcener is one who has a right to demand that the family property be divided and they be handed over their share in the property (or whatever assets the HUF has) in case he or she decides to part ways with the HUF.

Can An Unmarried Man Create An HUF?

No! He cannot, if you mean an HUF of which he seeks to be the Karta himself. He can very well be the member of the HUF of his father or grandfather, but to create his own HUF he has to wait till his marriage. Every Hindu, after birth becomes a member of an HUF.

Can A Female Be The Karta?

The answer can't be No in the light of the amendment in the Hindu Succession Act in 2005. An unmarried daughter, in the unfortunate event of her father passing away, will become the Karta of the HUF if she has no brother.

Can There Be An All-Female HUF?

Yes, there can be. Where a couple had only a daughter and the husband passed away, the mother and daughter both can continue the HUF.

Can HUF Become Partner In Any Business?

No! The HUF can never be a partner in a firm. HUF is undoubtedly a person within the meaning of the Indian Income Tax Act, it is however not a juristic person for all purposes and cannot enter into an agreement of partnership with either another undivided family or an individual.

Can HUF Pay Remuneration To Its Karta?

Yes, if a remuneration is paid to a Karta of the family under a valid agreement which is bonafide in the interest of an expedient business of the family and the payment is genuine and not excessive, such a remuneration must be held to be an expenditure laid out wholly and exclusively, for the purpose of the business and must be allowed as an expenditure.

Tax Benefit to HUF if it Invests in Real Estate

If you are a businessman or self-employed then you must prepare an HUF. If you have created an HUF, then always invest in real estate whether residential or commercial in the name of the Hindu Undivided Family because HUF attracts a similar tax exemption to that available to an individual tax payer in respect of self-occupied property under section 80C and Section 24. This implies that if you avail a housing loan for HUF, you can save ₹2 lakh in interest and ₹1.50 lakh in principal repayment.

If the Hindu Undivided Family gives its property on rent, it would also enjoy the deduction of 30% of the annual value by way of standard deduction from the rental income so received by it.

So friends, create an HUF today, so that you can avail the unlimited tax exemptions and benefits provided.

❑

6

House Rent Allowance (HRA)

This is the part of salary of the person who is employed in any job/service. The HRA generally depends on the kind of employment. Normally, it is 20 % of basic salary in government sector. HRA is generally provided by the employer so that the employee is able to pay his rent.

It is not provided to the employees

1. Who live in a house provided by the company.
2. Who avails the house lease facilities provided by the company.

Since HRA provides rental support to the employee, hence it has an income tax exemption up to a certain level. The person who lives in his own house does not get any rebate on HRA in income tax.

Calculation of Rebate On HRA

The income tax rebate on HRA is governed by the following factors:

1. Basic Salary of employee.
2. HRA received by employee.
3. The city in which he currently resides (metro/non-metro)
4. Actual amount paid as rent.

Example: (A): Mr. Naveen Sharma is living on rent in Mumbai and working in a consultancy firm. He is paying ₹20000/month for rent. His annual salary details are as follows.-

- Basic Salary: ₹480000.
- HRA Received: ₹240000.
- Medical Allowance: ₹15000.
- Other allowances: ₹150000.

Since Naveen lives in one of four metro cities (Mumbai, Delhi, Kolkata and Chennai)

1. 50 % of Annual Basic Salary --- ₹240000.
2. Actual amount paid in rent – 10% of Basic Salary

   [20000 x12 – 48000(10% of 480000)]= ₹192000
3. Actual HRA received --- ₹240000.

The exemption in HRA received will be ₹192000.

Since Mr. Naveen is receiving ₹240000 as HRA so ₹192000 from HRA will be exempted from tax calculation and ₹48000 (240000-192000) will be clubbed in taxable income.

Example: (B): If Naveen is living in a non-metro city like Jaipur than first point calculation will be as 40 % of Annual Basic Salary ₹192000. In this condition, exemption will be the same.

Example: (C): If Naveen decides to prepare a rent agreement of for a rent of ₹24000/month, the calculation will be as under:

1. 50 % of Annual Basic Salary--- ₹240000.

2. Actual amount paid in rent – 10% of Basic Salary[24000 x12 – 48000(10% of 480000)]= ₹240000
3. Actual HRA received----- ₹240000.

The exemption in HRA received will be minimum of the above mentioned three points up to ₹2,40,000/

So due to this forged receipt Mr. Naveen will get the entire HRA amount exempted from income tax. However, why should the landlord agree to such a proposition since this kind of a rental agreement will attract additional income tax on the landlord's income of ₹48000.

Central Board of Direct Taxes (CBDT) has taken certain steps to prevent such types of forgery.

- From the Financial Year 2013-14 all salaried people who avail the benefit of HRA and pay ₹1 lakh or above as rent have to submit PAN card of their landlords.
- If his landlord has no PAN card, then the employee has to submit an affidavit from landlord that his landlord has no PAN card. Moreover the employee has to provide the name and address of the landlord.
- With this rule, the income tax department can find out whether landlords pay income tax or not on the rent receivables.

So if you pay a rent of more than ₹1lakh per year always remember to submit the PAN Card of your landlord to your employer.

The Basics to Claim HRA

1. You can claim HRA if you are living in a city other than city where you have a house. The city you live in is also important (metro/non-metro)

2. If you pay rent to your spouse then you are not eligible for HRA exemption.
3. If you live with your parents and pay rent to them than you are eligible for HRA exemption. However, your parents should include to the rent paid by you in their income and pay income tax accordingly to their income slab.

The People Who Don't Get HRA

Generally, businessmen and self employed professionals also get benefits as per the section 80GG of income tax. Although they don't get HRA but they have certain benefits. They can get exemption up to ₹2000 per month.

Mr. Ramlal is a businessman in Kolkata and his annual income is ₹250000/.He is living on rent and paying rent of ₹5000/month. Since Ramlal lives in a metro city: 10 % of Annual Income—Rs 25000.

Actual amount paid in rent 5000 x12= ₹60000.

Since he is eligible for exemption of ₹2000/month so he will get exemption of ₹24000/year.

❑

7

Home Loan

Today, the dream of owning a house can be easily realized by availing a home loan. However, before you apply for a loan, you need to think about your budget.

Draw up a budget on the basis of your net monthly income and expenses, including your insurance premium and other monthly out flow of investments (like MF sips, ELSS). It is important to find out how much you will be able to spare every month for EMI. Apart from the EMI, you will also have to consider other expenses, such as housing society charges and maintenance fee. This is the first basic step for deciding home loan amount because paying EMI is a long term commitment.

The advantage of purchasing a ready-to-move-in house is that you will save on your rent, which in turn will help you to pay your EMI. If you are residing in employer provided accommodation then after shifting to your newly purchased house, you can avail the benefit of house rent allowance which will help you to pay your EMI.

So, before you apply for a loan you should consider your income and savings. Moreover, you will also have to think about how much EMI you can easily pay without compromising your life style. You may also think about your future income. Remember, if you purchase an expensive property, then you require more money and you have to pay more amount of EMI.

If you are buying a flat which is in the 'under-construction' stage, your financial liabilities will slightly increase as you will have to pay the monthly rent in addition to the pre EMI (interest amount only up to 18 months) until you get the possession of the flat. Calculate the EMI you can afford to pay without having to compromise on your other goals and present lifestyle. If you feel that you cannot afford a bigger house, then opt for a smaller property or postpone your entire plan for some years.

Budget (Maximum loan to be provided by a bank + your margin) When you purchase a property two kinds of funds are important

1. Your own money (margin) -- 10 to 25%
2. Bank Loan--- Normally all banks or housing finance companies provide 75 % to 90 % loan of property value.

The Reserve Bank of India has made it compulsory for all financial institutions, including banks, not to exceed 80% of the cost of a house while extending loans to homebuyers. So you will require a large sum as the margin (your share in buying a house/flat). For example, if you buy a house worth ₹40 lakh, you will have to pay 20% of the amount, or ₹8 lakh as margin money. However, for home loans of up to ₹30 lakh, banks/ housing finance companies can finance up to 90% of the total value of the house.

Applying for a Provisional Sanction Letter

First of all, you should find out the maximum amount of loan that you can borrow from bank. For this purpose, you should obtain a provisional sanction letter. In some metros, when you approach a builder, he demands the provisional sanction letter. We are all familiar with the fear and anxiety that we feel when applying for a loan. After all, it's the bank who decides whether we can own our dream home, our first car, or whether our children can pursue quality higher education. In short, the probability of a better life depends on the lender's decisions.

Bank decides to give you a loan on your home loan application after considering two factors.

A. Your income/ ability to repay loan.

B. Your CIBIL Score (your intention to repay loan/ your loan track record).

A. **Your Income/ Ability to Repay The Loan:** Your income from job/business as well as the income from other sources is the main criteria for loan amount.

Banks / housing finance companies consider following things:

(1) The sector you work in (Pharmacy, IT, Government Sector, Private Sector, MNCs.)?

(2) Your company profile, your job profile, your post, your salary, your work experience, age and family liabilities.

(3) Whether you are a professional (doctor, lawyer, CA, CFA & architect). Bank considers your work experience, your yearly returns, your financial condition, etc.

(4) If you are a businessman, then the lender examines your experience in a particular business, condition of

your business, your firm/company's balance sheet and profit loss statement.

(5) In all the cases, banks take into account your present lifestyle and the costs involved in maintaining it.

Norms which are applicable for businessmen as well as for salaried class.

You can purchase a house only if the bank sanctions your loan. A bank will only do so if your saving to debt ratio is 40:60. Suppose your gross monthly income is ₹60000 / and net monthly income is ₹50000 (since there may be deduction of income tax, GPF/NPS and some other salary deductions). Now as per 40:60 rules, 40 percent of your salary should be saved 40 %(₹24000) and the total amount available for deduction and paying the EMI will be 60% (Rs 36000). Now the amount available for EMI is ₹26000 {(60% part of salary (Rs 36000) -deduction (Rs 10000)}. It clearly implies that you can take a home loan which has an EMI of ₹26000.If you have a car loan which has an EMI of ₹8000, then bank will only consider the remaining amount of ₹18000 for EMI.

So, when applying for a home loan, it is better to prepay car loan so that it does not create any problems in the sanctioning of the home loan. So, it is essential to free yourself from loans and have a healthy credit record before you take a loan. In case of businessmen, loan amount is decided on the basis of their average of ITRs filed in the last three years. Normally, every lender has a loan calculator on its official web site where you may calculate your loan amount. Some banks have different criteria to calculate home loan eligibility like borrower track record, turnover in business, average balance in account, etc.

How to Get More Loan Amount?

1. Salary and ITR are two main considerations for loan eligibility. If your salary is likely to increase in near future (due to pay revision, promotion and joining of a new job) then apply after increment.

2. If you are a businessman and your upcoming ITR is more than that filed in the last year, then apply after you obtain the records of the increased ITR.

3. Always apply loan with a co-applicant who is currently employed or has some sort of an income (your spouse, father, mother, son and unmarried daughter).

4. Always maintain a bank account which shows a high average balance.

5. Always maintain funds in the account so that there are no chances of the cheque bouncing or being dishonored due to the lack of funds.

6. If the sanctioned loan amount is less than what you actually need, then tell the bank officer that after shifting in the new house/flat you will get HRA (normally 20% of basic salary). So monthly income will increase.

7. You may ask the lender that you can stop some regular investment (SIPs) to increase the loan amount due to this you can pay higher EMI.

B. **Your CIBIL Score (your intention to repay loan/ your loan track records):** Normally banks consider CIBIL report having score of 600 to 900. CIBIL score 800+ is considered as good score for loan criteria. CIBIL score shows track of repayment of your past loans as well as current/running loans. CIBIL Report also shows that how many inquiries you have done for loan purpose in the past. Are your all loans being repaid timely? Is there any settlement/write off case? How much is your current liability and overdue if any? You may also apply for CIBIL Score on CIBIL website. Ultimately it is a best tool for bankers to know your intention to repay loan with loan liabilities. It also plays an important role for deciding rate of interest on housing loans. Some banks charges lower interest rate from the customers who have CIBIL Score more than 800.

How you can maintain a good CIBIL Score?

1. Always pay EMI on time.
2. Don't inquire for a loan unless you really need one.
3. If you are a credit card defaulter due to any reason, then settle / repay the credit card as soon as possible. In case you pay off the entire amount, your score will increase and bank or housing finance company may consider your application.
4. If you have overdue amounts in any loan then pay off the overdue amount as soon as possible.
5. In case you have not availed any loan so far, take some small loans for purchasing motorbike, fridge, TV, etc. It will help create your score. Once you repay or start repaying them, apply for home loan.
6. Normally avoid giving a personal guarantee to any person until it is necessary, because if the applicant does not pay the EMI on time then it decreases your CIBIL score.
7. It may happen that you have opted for a loan at a floating interest rate. The floating interest rate may increase which in turn causes the EMI to increase. You may not be aware of the increase and keep paying

the old EMI. The increased amount may reflect as the overdue amount which may impact your CIBIL score.

Credit Information Report

While there are many factors that affect your loan application, the most important is your Credit Score or your Credit Information Report. Now a days, almost all banks and NBFCs access your Credit Score to evaluate and approve your loan application. Since your Credit Score is a very important part of the loan application process and is derived from your Credit Report, it is very important that you have an in-depth understanding of your CIR. CIR includes the following five aspects:

1. **Personal information:** This contains your personal information such as your name, date of birth, gender, identification number (e.g. PAN, Voter ID or Passport Number, Driving License, etc.)

2. **Contact Information:** This is the next field to fill. Your current, as well as permanent residential addresses with telephone numbers are provided in this section.

3. **Employment Information:** This section provides the lender information about your monthly or annual income which may include details as reported by borrower. The reported income is generally the figure you declared during loan application and will not necessarily be your latest income.

4. **Account Information:** The account information contains information about your credit cards, debit cards, loans. It also has a detailed history of transactions conducted by you which includes payment defaults, payment patterns and over-due amounts.

5. **Inquiry Information:** Inquiry is done from three people who are in the same line.

A Good Deal for Home Loan

Question: Where to apply?

Answer: Apply where the rate of interest is lower as compared to market or there is a relaxation in other overheads. Moreover, apply in a place where people treat the customers well before and after the home-loan approval.

First of all, compare the rate of interest of all the banks. Normally the rates of all home loan providers are almost equal. Look at the other overhead charges and compare them. You may also approach the bank where your salary is credited.

Always inquire from the old borrowers about their experience with the banks or housing finance companies. Preferably choose a bank where you have a good relationship with the manager. If you are a businessman then you should prefer a bank where you already have a term loan or have a cash credit limit. See whether the project you are investing in is approved by your bank or not. It's a good idea to opt for a loan on floating rate of interest because it has no prepayment charges. When you book a flat in a group housing project then inquire from the sales executives whether they have any tie-ups with banks for loans.

Arrangement for Margin Money / Your Share in Purchase Price

Now I am going to tell you the best way to arrange margin money for your dream house. After joining your first job in any organization, you should start saving a fraction of your income over a period of 4-5 years. In this period of time you may be bachelor or may just be married or may have had children. Even if you have small children, generally expenses are very low in this period, so you can save a lot of money by investing in various financial instruments. In case you follow this plan, probably by the age of 28 to 30 years you should be ready to buy your own house.

However, if you have not invested or saved in the early years of your career and are planning to buy a house, you can avail any of the following options to ensure margin money for your house.

- Employees may take loan from their employers like loan against PF. You may also partially or fully withdraw your provident fund amount. Some organizations provide bridge loans for their employees at lower rate of interest.
- If you have gold ornaments then you may take loan against these ornaments or even sell them if they are not being used.
- If you have a piece of land, whose price is not appreciating as per your expectation or you don't want build a house on it, then you should sell it. People who live in the cities and have agricultural land in their villages can sell the land in case they don't need it or do not visit the village any longer.
- Liquidate your investments (like mutual fund, shares, recurring deposits, FD, etc.), which are not paying returns matching your home loan interest rate.
- You can take personal loan from other banks or financial institutions, but it should not create any extra burden on your finances. Remember, you should apply for both personal loan and home loan at the same time otherwise it may affect your eligibility for either of the loans. Taking any kind of loan on your credit card is not a good idea as the exorbitant interest rates could lead you into a debt trap.
- If you have availed a home loan within the last two years, then you may take a top-up loan, which can be used as margin money for new housing loan.
- You may take loan against your PPF account if it is more than three years old.
- Loan may be taken against life insurance policies.

- You may also take help from your close friends or relatives depending on your relationship with them
- You may be someone who has taken care of all their financial liabilities such as their children's education or marriage and have their own house and have a great job or business. In this situation, in case your children or their spouses are planning to purchase a house, you can think about helping them. Now-a-days the property prices are sky high and young people do not have as many savings to fall back upon. However, this does not mean that the children should look up to their parents to finance their investments. This should be clearly considered as a help and the entire amount should be repaid within a specific deadline.

Remember that buying a house shouldn't throw a spanner in other important long-term life plans, such as your child's higher education or your own retirement.

Sometimes you may face a problem where suppose you finalize a house deal for ₹50,00,000/. At that time seller tells you that he would take ₹20,00,000/ in cash and will do registry for the amount of ₹30,00,000/. This means that as far as a bank is concerned, your sale consideration is only ₹30,00,00/, which is mentioned in the agreement to sale and the sanctioned loan will be ₹27,00,000/. The seller wants to save his capital gain tax and hence wants to do the registry for the minimum amount possible. If you listen to the seller, you will end up losing an opportunity to avail more loans, which could have helped you to meet all your seen and unseen expenses.

Remember:

1. If you are taking a home loan for construction of house then always opt for maximum home loan; because when you construct your house during construction period, your

budget may increase. Always try to make construction estimate 25% extra rather than actual required.

2. When you are applying for a housing loan then apply for maximum tenure (loan period); because in case your expenses increase or you take another loan in the future, you will be able to cover these expenses and also pay the EMI as per your convenience.

❑

8

Joint Home Loan

In India, home loan is becoming popular amongst the masses. Rise in living standard is main reason for real estate development in India. Home loan also helps in saving a substantial amount of income tax.

What Is Joint Home Loan?

This is a loan taken on single property by two or more people jointly. Normally in this type of a home loan, the property may have two or more owners. At times, there are only single owner and a co-Applicant is added to increase the loan amount.

Who Can Be Co-borrower in Home Loan?

Spouse, son, father, mother and unmarried daughter can be co-borrowers in a loan.

In case the property is purchased by two brothers (siblings) then the bank might approve their joint home loan since both will be the co-owners of the property.

Occasionally friends, sisters and unmarried couples can be co-owners in a property but generally they are not considered as co-borrowers. Some banks or housing finance companies may consider these types of cases on a case-to-case basis.

However, a rule, banks do not prefer to give loans to two friends or two relatives (cousins etc.) because there are chances that they may have disagreements and disputes in the future which may lead to court cases etc.

Is It Compulsory To Be Co-owner In Property For Joint Home Loan?

No, it is not compulsory. The difference between a co-applicant and co-owner is that the latter has a share in the property, while a co-applicant is simply liable for repaying the loan in case the primary applicant is unable to service it.

In relationships like son-father, son-mother and husband-wife co-ownership is not mandatory. However, it is mandatory in certain cases.

For example incase a father and his unmarried daughter are purchasing a property and want a home loan, then both of them should be the co-owners of the property. When two brothers, two friends and distant relatives take home loan then they must be co-owner of property. Generally, the maximum number of co-applicants allowed in most of the banks and finance companies is six. Here it must be kept in mind that the maximum repayment period considered by a bank is 70 years. The repayment period is determined by the age of the oldest co-applicant. Suppose father is 55 years old and son is 30 years old, then bank will sanction a loan for a period 15 years.

Can All Co-borrowers Avail The Benefit Of Income Tax Exemption?

Yes!

All co-borrowers can avail the benefit of income tax exemption, but it is compulsory that co-borrowers should be the co-owners of the property and loan should be repaid by each co-applicant.

If all co-borrowers are co-owners in the property then benefit under section 80C/24 of income tax will be decided on their individual portion of loan repayment amount.

What are the Benefits of Joint Home Loan?

1. All co- borrowers can avail maximum benefit of 80C (Repayment of principal up to ₹1,50,000/per co-borrower if property is self occupied.) and Section 24 Repayment of interest up to ₹2,00,000/per co-borrower if property is self occupied.
2. When you require a larger loan amount you are advised to club a co-applicant in loan so that the bank can increase your loan amount.

CASE STUDY

Mr. Ram Jeet Singh is an officer in Rajasthan Government. Few years back, he purchased an open plot of Jaipur Development Authority in his wife Mrs. Dipali's name. Mrs. Dipali is getting income from private teaching and coaching classes. They decided to build a double storey house on that plot. Both approached a nationalized bank for home loan. They wanted a home loan of ₹20 lakh but Mrs. Dipali's income was not sufficient to avail home loan of desired amount. Bank officer suggested that in case they club their incomes together they will be able to avail the desired loan amount. The loan was sanctioned in joint names. Within one and half year their dream house was ready for possession.

However, at the time of purchasing the plot Mr. Ram Jeet Singh committed a mistake. Do you know what the mistake was?

He purchased the property in only his wife's name. However, this is a common mistake made by millions of Indians.

Why?

1. People are not familiar with income tax laws.
2. In many states stamp duty for purchasing a property is lower in case of a woman. Hence to avoid a higher stamp duty, people purchase property in the woman's name who is generally a housewife in most Indian families.
3. Many employees or businessmen don't want to disclose their property since they may have used black money for buying the property.

Now, let's get back to our case study. Ram Jeet and Dipali both were repaying the loan from their joint accounts. Then, at the time of filing their income-tax returns, Ram Jeet wanted to deduct all the interest payment paid by him as co-applicant in the house property while computing his taxable income. For this purpose he obtained interest certificate from bank. The bank may issue interest certificate to both applicants without considering their ownership but mention some line of income tax law. It may be noted here that under the provisions of the Income-tax Act, 1961 any individual who takes loan for residential house property after 1st April, 1999 is entitled to deduct interest on loan for self-occupied house property to the maximum extent of ₹2,00,000 per individual. This provision was very well known to Ram Jeet and Dipali so both of them decided to claim the deduction in respect of interest on loan as well as a tax deduction in respect of repayment of the principal amount of the loan under Section 80C of the Income-Tax Act, 1961.

This is generally the case with a lot of young and earning couples. They take a joint loan, pay the interest and principle amounts together and also avail the benefit of tax deductions. However, in this case, Ram Jeet Singh was unable to enjoy any tax benefit despite being a co-borrower.

Why?

The answer is very simple. Dipali was the single owner of the plot on which the house was built. Since Ram Jeet was not the owner of the plot, he did not have a legal right in the immovable property for which he has taken loan. In the absence of a legal title; the benefit in respect of interest deduction as well as by way of tax rebate on repayment of housing loan could not be extended to Ram Jeet. The matter did not end here. Dipali in any case could also not enjoy full tax deduction in respect of interest on loan paid by her husband. She could only enjoy half of the interest which she has paid. The benefit also depends on the share of repayment in the loan. From the case history of Ram Jeet and Dipali, we can conclude that it is never a good idea to make another family member as a co-applicant or borrower in the loan when the land/building belongs to only one person. So it is a good idea to purchase property jointly rather than singly. So, if you purchase a property along with your other family members all the co-owners can take home loan and take other benefits of income tax individually of joint property ownership.

Coming back to Ram Jeet's problem, the only way to rectify the mistake was to purchase half of the building portion belonging to Dipali. Now it is clear that Ram Jeet had to execute a sale deed buying out half portion of the house belonging to Dipali. This allowed him to become the legal co-owner of the house which would then allow him to enjoy tax benefit on the interest payment as well as principal payment made by him as a co-borrower. However, the disadvantage here is that Ramjeet had to pay the stamp duty as per state stamp act. Moreover, when property is mortgaged with bank, he was not permitted to sell the property. It is a good idea to learn from the mistakes of other people so that you don't commit the same mistake. You know that real estate investment is a long term investment, hence be careful and always seek guidance from tax advocates, financial planners, bankers or your friends and relatives who have sound knowledge of tax planning in real estate investment.

Should You Take A Home Loan Jointly With Your Spouse?

Have you and your spouse decided to buy a house with the help of a joint home loan? Exciting as the prospect of purchasing a house seems to a married couple, they need to consider both the advantages and drawbacks of taking a joint loan.

Benefits

- **Bigger loan:** Compared with an individual loan limit, you will be eligible for a higher loan as a couple. So if your individual eligibility for a loan may be ₹30 lakh, combined with the spouse's limit of, say, ₹20 lakh, your combined loan limit could go up to ₹50 lakh and you may be able to buy a bigger house.
- **Concessions:** With several banks offering lower interest rates to women applicants; it could help to have the wife as a primary applicant for the home loan. Similarly, the stamp duty fee for registration of the house is lower for women and couples, varying marginally in different states.
- **Tax benefit:** We have already discussed it.

Drawbacks

- **Divorce or death:** In case of differences or a split between the spouses, loan repayment can become a sore point. If the wife is only a co-applicant and the husband stops paying the EMIs, the burden of repaying the entire loan fall on the wife without the benefit of ownership. Even in case of death, the surviving spouse will have to shoulder the repayment. In case of non-repayment, the lender has the right to seize the assets of a co-applicant.
- **Limited share:** If the husband dies without a will and the wife is only a co-applicant, she will only get one-third share of the property as a legal heir, since the asset will be split among parents, wife and children of the deceased.
- **Eligibility & credit score:** If the partners are joint applicants and a spouse refuses to pay the home loan EMI, the credit score of both will be affected equally. Similarly, their eligibility for a loan in the future will be impacted in case of a default.

Safeguards

- **Insurance:** To ensure that the burden of home loan does not fall on one partner in case of death or divorce, it is a good idea for the primary applicant to buy a term insurance plan and include the home loan liability in the cover.
- **Agreement:** In anticipation of differences in the future, the spouses should sign an agreement specifying the share of loan liability of each partner in case of a dispute, and have it notarized.

❑

9

Home Saver Loan

Forty-two year old Naveen has booked a flat and now he is searching for the best home loan deals. Some of his friends told him about Home Saver Loan. Now, Naveen is facing a dilemma common to many flat/house buyers and wondering whether he should opt for home saver or not. He is wondering whether to prepay and save interest on the home loan or save the money for rainy days. The urge to prepay at least a part of the principal is strong. At the same time, he is worried about the liquidity crunch in the event of any contingency that may crop up soon after deploying his funds. Perhaps he doesn't really know about the best choice.

For all those wanting to have their cake and eat it too, banks offer a product called home saver loan. In the basic housing loan product, once a loan is fully disbursed i.e. once there is no available limit remaining, no further withdrawal/debit is permitted to the loan account. In fact, even if you repay more than the scheduled requirement i.e. when you have cash surplus and you want to pay off some percentage of the loan,, no further withdrawal/debit is permitted at a later date. Let us say that you have a loan of ₹25 lakh having EMI of ₹24000 and outstanding amount is ₹24 lakh. If you deposit ₹5 lakh in the loan then new outstanding will be ₹19 lakh. But friends, in basic home loan you cannot withdraw excess amount paid by you for any emergency. This means that if any point of time if you have surplus funds and use them to reduce the outstanding of the home loan, those funds won't be available to you in future. Thus, such reduction in outstanding of the loan account is at the cost of reducing the personal liquidity in the future as the funds which were used to prepay the loan would otherwise have been available to the borrower.

This problem can be overcome by availing the option of home saver, an innovative and customer friendly product for customers which enables them earn an optimal yield on their savings by reducing interest rate burden on home loans, with no extra cost. This facility allows the borrower to deposit his excess savings in a current account linked to his home loan account. While calculating the interest component, the bank deducts the balance in the current account from the borrower's outstanding principal. Typically, the average monthly balance in the account is considered for this purpose. Meanwhile, the money can be easily withdrawn in case of an emergency. The only drawback is that in case of a home saver loan, some banks charge about 0.25-0.50% more interest rate than regular home loans. The loan is sanctioned as an overdraft with added flexibility to operate the home loan account like savings bank and current account. For this bank also provides cheque book and internet banking facility for borrowers. In some banks, the borrower needs to give instruction for withdrawal of the excess fund from housing loan account as and when required.

At present, this facility is being offered by leading players like the State Bank of India (Maxgain), Union Bank of India (Smart Save), IDBI Bank, Citibank, Punjab National Bank

(PNB Flexible Housing Loan), Standard Chartered Bank and HSBC.

The home saver loan suits everybody. Since it is advisable as a part of financial planning to maintain nearly six months worth of household expenses as a contingencies corpus, people can park this amount in the linked current account and avail dual benefits. The contingency fund could range from ₹3-10 lakh, especially in households with dependent parents. We also include medical contingencies in this corpus. Imagine the amount you could save off your outstanding principal with this corpus parked in a current account linked to a home saver loan account.

What are the Benefits?

The money in the linked current account not only helps reduce your interest burden, while remaining easily accessible, but is also safe from the taxman. Moreover, though this balance is treated as part payment, the bank does not impose any prepayment penalty for the same. Even if you do not foresee a windfall coming your way, you can choose to avail this product by simply depositing a part of your salary as a recurring amount in your current account. Let's says if you have a regular home loan of ₹40 lakh and you have prepaid ₹10 lakh. Now on Diwali you want to purchase a car and for this you decide to take a loan from the bank. However, please note that a car loan has a higher interest rate associated with it. Instead you can use the home saver loan overflow amount for purchasing the car. Moreover, this extra amount may also be useful to cover the expenses related to the higher education and marriage of your children.

What are the Limitations?

As mentioned earlier, home saver loans are more expensive than regular home loans. Secondly, the deposit in the current account doesn't generate any interest income. If you were to invest this money in mutual funds or equity, you'd earn much higher returns. So, this option is primarily for those, for whom liquidity is a primary concern.

As with any financial product, the rule of thumb is to shop carefully for the best deal since interest rates differ from bank to bank. However, be aware that the eligibility criteria will also vary. A borrower must take the time to understand the math involved in home saver loans and the various charges associated with it before rushing to buy this product. For example, if you have taken a regular home loan of ₹25 lakh with regular EMIs and you have ₹5 lakh as excess cash. In case of a regular home loan, you may prepay the loan, but you cannot withdraw this excess amount at a later date. However in case of a home saver you will always be tempted to spend these funds or you may use the money in unnecessary things like purchasing a car on Diwali even when you don't need it.

❑

10

Home Loan Transfer or Other Option

One day I was sitting with an old friend Dr. Sachin Gupta who is an orthopedic surgeon at Shekhawati Hospital, Jaipur. During the conversation he told me that he had a housing loan of ₹20 lakh from a bank which was at an interest rate of 8.75% p.a. At that time, the normal housing loan interest rate offered by banks was around 7.00 to 7.25%. Moreover, the bank from which he had taken the loan was offering a lower interest rate to its new customers. I suggested him to transfer the home loan immediately to a lender who could offer the loan at a lower rate of interest. These days, most borrowers transfer their home loans from one lender to another because of a significant difference between the rates that their bank/housing finance company is charging its old customers vis-a-vis the one being levied on the new customers.

A difference in rates might also arise between your lender and others. If there is a significant difference you can save a lot of money and a shift is advisable. Some customers may find it difficult to pay the higher EMI; they may want the lender to increase the tenure and reduce the installment. If their current lender refuses, the customers can look for another lender. Poor service standards may also a reason for shifting. However, that may not be so relevant since once you take the home loan, all you will contact the bank for is the annual interest certificate which is required for tax calculations.

Let us say you have identified a lender who offers a lesser rate of interest and you'd like to transfer your home loan. However, before you do anything, it is advisable to have a meeting with present lender. Because now-a-days, thanks to the cut-throat competition, no lender wants to lose customers. They may either lower the interest rate of the loan without any additional charges or they may advise you to deposit 0.25 to 0.50% of the charges to convert the higher interest rate to current interest rate (the lower rate which is being charged from new customers). This may be a good option rather than shifting. All lenders normally increase the rate of interest of home loan when RBI increases its Repo Rate and decrease it when the Repo Rate is decreased. However, there are some lenders who don't decrease rate of interest even when RBI decreases its Repo Rate which means they always have a high rate of interest. Shift your home loan from such type of lenders.

How do you know whether the lender is charging the right rate of interest? First of all, observe the track record of the loan for one year or at least six months. You can ask for the foreclosure letter which shows the outstanding principal of your home loan with interest amount up to a particular date.

In case you are thinking of transferring the home loan to a new lender, ensure that you collect the list of the required documents from the present lender because the new lender will ask you to submit photocopies of all the documents issued by present banker. Submit all these papers to the new lender, who will then do all formalities like legal and valuation of property, contact point verification of your office and residence and CIBIL. After sanction of a new loan, the new lender will issue a demand draft to your old lender to close the loan account. Original papers of the property will be released from the old lender and will be deposited in custody of new lender. New lender will charge stamp duty (according to State Stamp Act), processing charges, and property insurance charges.

Friends, remember to always maintain good track record of repayment since it plays a major role in loan transfer. If there is some default in your track record, let the new banker know the real reason behind the delay or the non-payment of the EMI. In this condition, loan transfer solely depends on discretion power of loan manager of new bank. Normally the new lender is not concerned with margin of the loan because the previous lender has already got the margin from the customer. It means if you have an outstanding home loan of ₹27 lakh, then the new lender will take over ₹27 lakh. If a property (normally a flat in a multistoried building) is under construction then it should be in the list of pre-approved projects of new lender.

Make sure that the bank to which you plan to transfer your loan should have lower interest rate by at least 25 to 50 basis points from present lender. If the difference is just 0.10% to 0.25 % then it is not advisable to transfer a loan where the amount is less than or equal to ₹25 lakh. But if loan is more than ₹50 lakh then transfer the loan. So, if your loan has an interest rate of 7.50% and new lender is offering a rate of 7.25%, do not shift the loan if it is below ₹25 lakh. Also ask the new lender about legal, valuation, insurance and other charges, and bargain for waiver of processing charges. Now-a-days banks don't charge prepayment penalty on loans that are on floating rate of interest.

Other Option or Make the switch in time

If your home loan is linked to your bank's MCLR or to its base rate, you are probably paying a high rate of interest. On 1 October 2019, all banks shifted to the Reserve Bank of India mandated external benchmarks (Repo Rate) for pricing their new home loans. So most banks now offer loans linked to the repo rate. This rate is called as EBLR (External Benchmark Lending rate). Banks have to reset the rates in every three months. You should get your loan linked to the repo rate. Existing borrowers who are servicing MCLR or Base Rate-linked loans can switch over to the external benchmark-linked loans after paying administrative or legal charges. The final rate and other terms and conditions will be similar to those for new borrowers in the same category. Most of the banks allow borrowers to switch after paying 0.25% of the outstanding loan amount as conversion fee. So before shifting the loan to another bank, discuss the process of lowering the rate of interest.

❑

11

Tax Saving Tricks for Home Loan

When you take a home loan, you must remember the provision of Income Tax Act 1961. When we purchase a house/flat, construct a house, and renovate a house, if we take home loan for above mentioned activities, then we are eligible for rebate under section 80C & 24 of Income Tax act 1961.

When we repay loan in the form of EMI? The EMI comprises of two parts: Interest and the Principal.

Interest Amount: If a person takes home loan to purchase residential property (not plot), then he is eligible for tax exemption under Section 24 of Income Tax Act.

1. If he occupies his house, its limit is ₹2 lakhs.
2. If he gives it on rent, then income in the house property head can't exceed ₹200,000/- after interest on loan in the negative side.

A. Self Occupied Property

In this condition, property is occupied by its owner. It is calculated as negative income from house. The reason is that according to Section 24 of the Income Tax Act, a deduction up to a maximum of ₹2,00,000 is allowed in respect of amount borrowed after 31.3.1999 for investment in self-occupied residential house property according to norms. This amount of deduction would result in a net loss up to ₹2,00,000 from "house property" and would be available for adjustment or set off against any other income like income from business, salary and income from other sources, etc.

If you have taken home loan, then you are entitled to income deduction u/s 24 @ ₹2,00,000 per person on account of Interest on housing loan. You are also eligible for deduction up to ₹1,50,000 under Section 80C of income tax for repayment of the principal of the loan. If you have taken home loan for renovation, reconstruction of house then the amount under section 24 will be ₹30,000/only.

After marriage, a total amount of ₹4 lakh of interest on loan for self-occupied one single property will be allowed by way of deduction, namely to the extent of ₹2,00,000 per person. Thus, it is only after marriage when you buy property jointly in your name and your spouse's name that you can claim deduction on the entire interest amount of ₹4 lakh. Similarly, when your wife is the co-owner in the property and she also makes payment of the loan taken from the bank, then the repayment of the loan is again admissible as a deduction within the overall limit of ₹1.5 lakh being deduction under Section 80C. You can avail of deductions on both, interest and principal repayments on a home loan, subject to a few conditions. The deduction on interest is limited to ₹2 lakh per year in case of a self-occupied property, but there is a condition that if this property is not acquired or constructed within three years of the end of the financial year in which the loan was taken, the benefit gets reduced from ₹2 lakh to ₹30,000 only.

Now days, when possession delays are rampant, this is a risk that all buyers have to face. Friends, if you would like to take advantage of this important deduction of the income-tax law, ensure that you should not own more than one self-occupied residential property because under the provisions of the Income Tax Act, only one self-occupied house property is completely exempt from being taxed on its notional rental value. So if you have two houses, use only one for self-occupation and let out the other house. This benefit is not available for commercial or industrial property.

B. Property Given on Rent

If you give a property on rent, then income in the house property head can't exceed ₹200,000/- after interest on loan in the negative side.

If you have two (more than one) houses on which you have availed home loan.

(One is self occupied and other is on rent.)

In this situation, you can consider only one house as self-occupied and other should be considered on rent even when it is actually given on rent or not.

1. **HOUSE NO. 1:** Home Loan interest is ₹160000 (given on monthly rent of ₹20000)

i.	Rental Income from it	₹ 240000
ii.	Less: Std. Deduction (30%)	₹ 72000
iii.	Net Income	₹168000
iv.	Less: Interest on Loan	₹160000
v.	Net taxable	₹ 8000

2. **HOUSE NO 2:** Self Occupied Interest on Home Loan-₹240000

   Total of House 1 and 2 +8000-240000= - ₹232000

But maximum allowed deduction in one year is up to 2.00 lakh so ₹2.00 lakh is to be set off in current year and remaining ₹32000 will be carried forward for next years (up to 8 years)

C. Supposed/Deemed Tax on Rent

Suppose you have a house in which you are living. Now, let us say that you purchase another house and it is vacant after purchasing. You have taken a home loan on each of these houses.

The first house, in which you are living, is eligible as per self-occupied house. However, in case of the second house which is vacant, would be treated as 'on rent'.

House /Flat Under Construction

You should remember one most important consideration is that the acquisition of a flat (in a case where you purchase an under-construction flat from a builder) or the construction of the residential house should be completed within three years of the purchase. If you fulfill these two important conditions then the investment in residential house property will be a tax haven for the investors like you.

The deduction on interest is available from the year in which the construction is completed. Any interest paid earlier can be deducted in five equal annual installments beginning from the year of completion. Such a claim is also subject to the limit of ₹2 lakh or ₹30,000 for a self-occupied property. Section 80C also allows a deduction of up to ₹1.5 lakh per year on principal repayments. But friends, keep in mind that this benefit is subject to the condition that the property was held for five years from the end of the year in which possession was obtained. If you sell this property within five years, then the benefit would be reversed.

❑

12

Invest the Surplus or Repay the Existing Home Loan?

This is a question that never has an off-season. Here's a typical example. Last week a customer of my branch asked me that he has a home loan on which he is paying an interest of 7.50 % a year. There's no problem—he is able to pay the EMI comfortably out of his salary income. However, he now finds that he also has some cash accumulated which he can invest. He wanted to know what the better option was: Repay some of his home loan outstanding amount before schedule, or invest the money in an equity mutual fund for the long-term.

This is a common dilemma. In fact, it's possible that practically every salary earner who takes a housing loan faces it at some point. You take a loan at an EMI you can afford. Eventually, your income increases and you find that can pay back more of the loan than you had originally planned.

If you were to ask this question of a financial planner, the chances are that he would tell you to repay the loan first. That advice is based on what is a first principle of personal financial planning—clear your debts before you save.

That principle is a sound one and should almost always be followed. As a banker I said 'almost' always. If the choice were between clearing expensive credit card debt/personal loan and saving, then clearly, one should do that. The same probably holds for most consumer loans, including big ticket ones like cars and such. This principle is most relevant to people who try to borrow and invest.

However, there are some caveats to the standard advice. On the face of it, long-term investments in an equity mutual fund will possibly fetch higher returns than the interest that savers are paying on housing loans. In the past, SIP returns have been higher for most 10-year periods. This situation is roughly true for everyone who is trying to save while servicing a housing loan.

In the case of a housing loan, the effective trade-off is even more in favor of not repaying the loan early because of the tax breaks one gets on the interest paid. If you compensate for that and calculate the real effective interest rate, then you'll find that your savings have to cross an even lower bar. The actual advantage you get from having taken the loan would also include the fact that you no longer have to pay rent. It's only when someone has built up a large enough financial saving that is liquid and accessible, and is in a situation where no great expense is anticipated that it would be justifiable to retire the loan instead of saving.

On top of that there's another side to this, which is human psychology. If someone has little or no savings at all, then no matter what the situation, no matter what the interest rates, he or she would prefer to carry the loan but have some savings. In such a situation, it would make sense to have access to the savings if they are needed, even if the savings are fetching the same or less returns than the one is paying on the debt one has taken. In the context of the COVID-19 pandemic in the year 2020, saving played an important role.

In other words, the rules for the first bit of saving you do—emergency money, so to speak—are different. Having instant access to an emergency fund is worth any kind of disadvantage that an interest rate differential brings.

❑

13

If you are Unable to Pay EMI

On 19th day of August 2013, I was facing an interview for the post of Senior Manager (Credit) in a leading public sector bank at Gurugram. During the interview session the panel came to know that I was experienced in retail loans. One of the committee members asked me a question, "Mr. Yogesh suppose you have a good housing loan borrower in your branch who is regularly paying EMI from last five years. Suddenly his EMI stops for one month after that it delays for more than 60 days. You call him regularly for paying the due EMI. One day the customer comes to your branch and told you that his father was admitted in a hospital from last five months. He also tells you that he has incurred a lot of expenses due to the treatment and has also lost his job due to the continuous absence from the job. He then states that he will not be able to repay the loan for the next six months. Moreover, he tells you that he and his family have only this house so he does not want to sell it. As you are a banker and know that if loan is not paid up to 90 days, it becomes as NPA (Non Performing Asset). And you have to conduct a recovery procedure with SERFASI Act. How you will react to the situation and how you will resolve it?"

Buying a house is the most expensive purchase you are likely to make in your life, so you may need help in the form of a loan to fund it. After taking home loan there may be several incidents which may disrupt your financial health like medical exigency (critical illness or accidents in the family), loss in business and loss of your job. These reasons deplete your savings. Since you have taken a housing loan, now it will be difficult for you to repay the loan EMI. Will the lender seize your property if you miss 2-3 EMIs? No, not immediately, but if you continue to default for six months, the bank will take over the possession of your house.

Banks don't give home loans to sell the dream home of a person. The attaching of a property is the last thing a lender wants to do. Though banks have the power to enforce the Securitization and Reconstruction of Financial Assets and Enforcement of Security Interest Act, 2002, (SARFAESI) to recover non-performing assets without the intervention of any court of law, this is the last step they prefer to take.

A bank usually allows a borrower to delay one EMI up to 30 days, but for the next one, it will remind you through letter or mail that you have overdue in your account and your EMIs are pending. After three defaults, the bank will send a demand notice, asking you to pay your dues as soon as possible. If the borrower doesn't respond to any of the mails, the bank sends a legal notice through its legal department.

A bank waits for three months before declaring an asset a non-performing one. After the end of this period, the bank can officially term the home loan as an NPA and start the process of recovering the property through the SARFAESI Act.

Even after invoking the Act, the bank gives the borrower a 60 days' notice period to repay the dues. Finally, five months after the first default, the bank publishes a notice in a local newspaper stating the location of the property, reserve price for auction and the date of auction.

Banks and financial institutions are more interested in recovering the money than in starting legal proceedings as the procedure of attaching and auctioning a house is lengthy and takes time. So, they will pursue the matter for at least six months before taking any legal action.

Steps to Take If You Miss The EMIs

- First of all, call your bankers and tell them the actual reason for delay in payments and reason for cheque bouncing.
- Now ask your lender to inform you about the options available.
- If the default is due to a hike in interest rates, ask the bank to reschedule the loan and increase the tenure to keep the EMI at the same level or reduce it.
- You can ask the bank to restructure your loan payment by taking into consideration the future income or by offering your savings as collateral.
- Make a chart that includes all your monthly mortgage payments. This will convince the bank that you have been a good customer who has been forced to default due to circumstances beyond your control.

If you are serious about paying your dues and have a good repayment track record, the bank will be willing to offer a leeway. The first step that the bank takes is to understand the reason for the default since a home loan is a secured one, with the bank having more control over the asset. If a bank is satisfied that the problem is genuine and that the borrower will start paying the EMI soon, it will be willing to wait for some more time. However, banks take such decisions on a case-to-case basis.

Most lenders take a practical view of the situation and understand how critical the house is for you. So they will closely interact with you and your family to understand the reason for the financial hardship. In fact, a bank will allow you to reclaim your property even after it has seized it, though this has to be done before the auction takes place. Even if the auction date has been announced, the borrower can come in at any stage and pay the dues to save his property. However, if the bank has incurred any charges for announcing the auction, the borrower will have to pay these charges.

What Are Your Options?

(My Answer to The Question Which Was Asked In The Interview.)

If you've lost your job, but are confident of getting a new one within six months, you can ask the bank to offer you a moratorium for this period. Request bank to reschedule the loan in such a way that up to six months you do not have to pay EMI and after that bank may increase EMI to cover the six EMIs. However, if your finances are strained due to some other reason, such as the EMI going up because of a hike in interest rates or increase in personal expenses, ask the bank to restructure your loan. In order to either reduce the EMI or keep it at the same level despite a higher interest rate, you could increase the loan tenure.

Prevention is Better than Cure

Friends, you should plan your savings such that you have at least six months of EMI amount as an emergency fund to fulfill the sudden demand for money. Some insurance companies also provide cover from critical illness and permanent total disability due to accident.

The main reason you need to start paying the EMI again, other than avoiding possession of your home by the bank, is to ensure that your credit score is not adversely affected. About 30% of your credit score is based on repayment history and a significant part of this usually depends on how regularly you repay your home loan, if you have taken one. Even one or two missed payments can negatively impact your credit score, and a continuous default will dent it severely, making it difficult to get loans or credit cards in the future. Since this is a dire circumstance, you could dip into your savings and retirement kitty and redeem your investments to pay the EMIs.

However, if it seems that the situation may not improve even after six months, a better idea may be to sell the property. You can talk to the bank about this and use the sale proceeds to prepay the loan. However, ensure that while the sale negotiations are on, you continue paying the EMIs. This will prove to the bank that you aren't taking it for a ride and will ensure that your credit score doesn't dip.

❑

14

Green Projects in Real Estate

Everyone loves saving an extra amount every month, but most people do not like cramping their lifestyle to cut costs. In a green building concept, one can save 30% electricity bill without compromising on their lifestyle. This implies that in green projects the electricity bills will be much lower. Hence as the owner of a green property you can avail the benefit of lower utility bills and nominal maintenance charges.

Normally people think that green buildings are more expensive, but in the long run one stands to gain by way of lower operating and maintenance costs. In every building almost 80-90% of the total cost of ownership of a building is attributed to operating and maintenance costs. In case of a green building, one can recover at least 50-55% of the initial premium one pays in the form of energy expenses within the next five years.

Green buildings have tremendous benefits. The immediate and most tangible benefit is in the reduction in water and operating energy costs. Evidence also shows that these features of energy-efficient buildings are translating into greater value in the form of increased rental rates, higher sale price, increased occupancy rates and lower operating expenses. But, installing these facilities also result in higher construction costs. In this way, green buildings have higher construction cost as compared to other normal buildings.

To qualify as a green project, certain specifications have to be met. Some features, such as the use of fly ash bricks to reduce pollution, use of high performance reflection glass, energy conservation lamps (led lights), water recycling and rainwater harvesting facilities, have to be incorporated in the project. These additional measures result in an increase in construction cost.

The incorporation of basic green features, if implemented in the right way at the preliminary design phase, should not influence your buying decision even if they appear to increase the initial cost of the project. Due to incorporation of these facilities an extra charge of only 51-55% is required. Some builders claim no increase in initial project cost due to their diligent planning.

Though some accessories and fixtures like ultra low-flow toilets and low flow sinks and shower heads, come at a premium, however once a building is complete one can reap the benefits like lower water consumption costs (by almost 50%). Moreover, these features allow you to claim additional incentives as decided by the local civic administration, which may include lower property taxes.

Recently, Union Bank of India has included installation cost of the solar plant in the construction cost of house. In this way, this public sector bank is promoting the go green concept. This is also beneficial for you if the power consumption in your house is reduced by 50-60% just by using appliances that use renewable resources such as solar power and are energy efficient. The design and layout plan of the project and the included individual buildings must be done in such a way that natural resources and sunlight are used in the most efficient way possible. This also reduces power bills.

Apart from energy-efficient and water conservation facilities, to get a green project rating a builder must also ensure passive architecture, optimal use of natural resources recycling plant, proximity to public transport, restored landscape and minimum disturbance to the site during construction. Projects are rated platinum, gold or silver, based on the various parameters, with platinum being the highest rating.

The construction cost would typically increase by 5-10% in a platinum-rated house, while gold or silver rating would increase the construction cost by 3-8%. The premium one has to pay for such projects while buying a house, however, is recovered within 3-5 years because of the lower maintenance and operating costs.

Should you Invest in Green Buildings?

National Building Construction Corporation Limited is also promoting green building concept by applying it in its residential projects. There's no doubt that you are going to benefit substantially from a green project if you are planning to buy a house for your own use. However, is a flat in green buildings a good investment option? Well, the concept of green buildings in India is still at a nascent stage. So, you have to choose your projects diligently. Although some experts say that rental rates could be higher by 2-15% and resale value can be improved by 5-30% for green projects, there are others who have a word of caution. They say, because of lack of awareness, one might have to wait longer to get a good resale price, considering the fact that other projects in the vicinity will come at a 10-15% discount as compared to green projects. Therefore, if you want to make quick money, it might not be a good idea yet. The financial benefits, however, whether they're realized cost savings or increase in productivity, are spurring the proliferation of green buildings.

❑

15

Now Start Your Search for a House or Flat

In the previous chapters you have understood a lot about the basics of real estate investment with a vast knowledge of home loan. From this chapter we will move in the next step of purchasing a house or flat.

In some cities where there are big industries or IT hubs; some employees have to take a decision to purchase a flat or live on rent. The question of whether you should choose to stay in a flat on rent or buy your own is one that troubles many.

Which is Fruitful: Renting or Buying

To solve this question you may take help of the Buy vs Sell Calculators which are available on some property selling websites like magicbricks.com. However, even the best calculators cannot give you the personalized advice that can serve you best when facing such a dilemma. The best solution is to logically think your problem in detail.

Everyone wants own a house. However keep in mind that you can only buy in a city or locality that matches your budget.

If you want the convenience of staying near your place to work, in a locality that matches your lifestyle needs and where you are close to friends or family, purchasing may not be the best option for you. Also, if the property rates are very high in that city, buying is often not the best option. You should live on rent.

For starters, do a SWOT - Strength, Weakness, Opportunity, and Threat-analysis. First, pin down the locality where you would like to stay and the type of house or flat you are looking for. Now identify an amount that you would be comfortable paying every month. If you find a house that you would like to stay in, which is close to your workplace is whether you can actually afford to buy in it your current circumstances.

There is a simple thumb rule, which is that the monthly repayment/ EMI must not be more than a third of your stable family income. That way you would be comfortable paying it back After all, you need to have enough money to manage your basic necessities and also be able to save a small bit while maintaining your existing lifestyle. Furthermore, when you decide to buy, you need to have margin money for home loan. Decide on purchasing only if these issues can be managed. Otherwise, take a house on rent and start saving towards that initial down payment.

Let me give you an example. Let's say you pay ₹10,000 as rent every month. If you find a flat that is suitable for your requirements and the EMI would be about 25 per cent more than your rental value, i.e. ₹2500 more per month, go for it and purchase the new flat. The outflow would require you to make a few lifestyle changes to be able to pay initially. But after some years as a result of annual salary increments, this 25 per cent extra will cease to be an irritant. Also remember that after taking this decision you are owner of a flat.

So friends, now I hope that you have taken a decision to buy a property after estimating your budget and selecting the city.

This book is based on the fact that you are purchasing the house for residential purpose.

Now in upcoming chapters we will discuss step by step on all the basic to buy a property.

OR

How to buy a Property?

For this purpose you have to follow the under mentioned steps.

1. Where should you buy/selection of the location?
2. Short listing of your property/selection of house or flat.
3. Property purchasing plans offered by developers.
4. Considering the different taxes on Real Estate that affect your budget.
5. Bargaining in Real Estate.
6. Agreement to sale.
7. Registry and possession.

Note: Always take a home loan from bank because before sanctioning,the bank does all due diligence of property and its seller. This exercise helps you to protect from fraud.

❑

16

Where Should you Buy? / Selection of Location

When you chose to buy a property, price is a good starting point. Your budget plays an important role in this process. Budget includes loan amount from the bank and cash in hand (margin) with you.

Start with your chosen budget and visit a property website such as Magicbricks.com, 99acres.com, OLX Homes and No Broker. Post your specifications in the search box and you will get a range of property options that match your requirements. Choose the size, the number of bedrooms required, and the amenities you are looking for and see which localities fit your requirements. See what you are comfortable paying. Then check out the location that offer you options within your budget. Of these, premium localities in downtown areas will be more expensive and you will have to settle for smaller units to fit your budget. As you move further away, you will get larger units as the per-square-foot price reduces.

There will always be a price difference between different locations that is proportionate to its strategic placement. For instance, if the unit is close to a bus stand /metro station or a flyover and therefore easily accessible, it will come at a much higher price than one that is more difficult to reach. Having good-quality water supply, regular power and access to transport services/ schools/ hospitals/ malls/ entertainment complexes push up values.

It is quite possible that particular area has good infrastructure, access to markets and places of entertainment but if it is loaded with existing and upcoming residential projects, then the price rises in that area may not be dramatic but a gradual one. Price depends on the gap between demand and supply. If the supply is more than demand then there will be a better chance of getting a good deal. On the other hand, if there is a greater demand and limited supply, it becomes a seller's market where sellers tend to hold values and there is little scope for negotiation as more buyers chase a smaller number of properties.

You can make an estimate of the number of available and proposed houses/flats in an area through a good property dealer and ascertain the past price movement in the short term. You can also check online at property portals to assess the number of properties that are listed for sale in that area. While finalizing the location of your property, these are the things you should keep in mind.

- Finalize your budget first and get a provisional sanction letter from the bank.
- The location should be within the approved or sanctioned master plan of the local development authorities.
- It should have good connectivity and there should not be significant chronic problems such is traffic jam within the micro-location or water logging during the rains. How well is the locality linked to metro station/bus stand, highways and flyovers or even to main sector roads? Sometimes if you are close to a metro station but are separated from the

station by a crowded U-turn, you may lose out on value. A critical factor you have to consider when buying a house is the time taken to travel to your place of work, essential areas such as schools, hospitals, and market and entertainment hubs as well as to other parts of the city where your friends or relatives may live.

- Infrastructure such as power, water supply, drainage and sewerage should be in place.

❑

17

Shortlisting of Your Property/Selection of House or Flat

After selection of the location in a city, the next step is to find out the best property in the selected location within your budget. Start narrowing down your options to the property that is the best match on online portal. Now start calling the agents or landlords who have posted the property on online portals. Some sellers and property dealers publish advertisements for selling properties in news papers especially in the Sunday edition. Some reputed dealers are also available and can be contacted via internet directories or some have their own website. You may also contact property dealers in a particular area; tell them your budget and location of property. Visit the property if you can as that gives you the best feel of what it would be like to stay there. If the place is ready for possession, talk with the people residing in the neighborhood. They will give you the real picture on what it is like to stay in that area.

Try and drive from that location to your place of work, to your child's school, market and other places you are likely to visit often. This will help you gauge how convenient the location is. If you are buying from the secondary market, visit and assess the kind of people living there. The neighborhood is very important as those are the people you will be interacting with the most when you stay there. Many people have come to grief because they bought the best possible property but did not factor in noisy or otherwise unsuitable neighbors. The quality of services available in the neighborhood also depends on the type of neighbors you have. Whatever is in demand is what will be available.

There is a wide range to choose from today as the market abounds in various housing formats-from 1, 2, 3 and 4BHK (Bedroom-Hall-Kitchen) apartments to studios, villas and row houses to builder floors and independent houses.

Deciding to purchase, determining your choice and then purchasing a house may seem daunting at first. However, approach the exercise scientifically and make sure you are driven by facts and information. After all, it is your money, your property and your lifestyle that is at stake. The best way to ensure that you have made the right choice is to do your own research. Use the data that is available online or offline and then go and check the sites on your own. Take charge and move forward. You will find that being armed with the right information can make the whole exercise enjoyable and fulfilling.

If you are not a good negotiator then you may take help of a broker or a lawyer or a friend or a relative, who is an expert in bargaining. In most cases, with a bit of research and running around, you can take the decisions on your own. However, if you do not have the time or not living in the city or the town where you wish to purchase the property, hiring these specialists may be a good idea.

How to Choose a Good Broker

There are some important aspects you need to consider when choosing a broker. Besides simplifying your home search, your real-estate agent will help evaluate the proposals that you get and choose the most profitable one. Use caution while you choose.

- Find out as much as possible about the agent before hiring his services. Ask for references. Also, ask family and friends to recommend real estate agents they have worked with.
- Ensure that all agreements between your agent and you have been put on paper.
- Do not pay money upfront to your real-estate agent. This could be a loss to you if you don't buy or sell a property through this agent. The agent's fee is paid after the deal is concluded and registered. You can pay agents by cheque but many ask for the amount in cash.

If you are planning to buy property through a broker, then you have to pay 0.5-2 per cent of the deal value, depending on the size of the deal. In lease transactions, the brokerage value is one month's rental or 8.33 per cent of the deal.

If you are Searching for an Individual House or Property

Friends, when you are purchasing an open plot or house, always prefer a loan from the bank whether you have money or not. The reason for it is that when bank is involved in a property, bank officers will also do due diligence of property and bank lawyer will examine the property documents. And another benefit is that bank will also check CIBIL Mortgage of property. CIBIL Mortgage will also tell you if that particular property is mortgaged with any other bank or not. These days every bank has to enter the property details in CERSAI, which has the full address of property with owner's detail along with the PAN.

If you are Searching for a Flat in a Multi-storey Apartment

First of all, finalize your budget and then select your preferred location, before selecting an apartment. Also consider your family size (number of family members at present and in near future) before selecting the flat. The other main points to be considered are builder's reputation, developer's financial strength, title of land on which apartment is being constructed, land acquisition, approvals from concerning authorities, payment plans, etc.

Multi-storey buildings and townships with all amenities in one project-clubhouse, health club, meditation centre, swimming pool, departmental store, school, cinema, sports facilities and banquet/party halls are what most end-users are looking at today. However, only a site visit can establish if the developer has given you more bedrooms but of smaller size. Sometimes you may want a more open layout and may be willing to sacrifice a bedroom for bigger sizes in the remaining units.

If you are buying into a new area as an investor, remember you will get best results only if you enter early in the cycle. If you enter too late, then the first mover advantage is lost and you may not be able to exit the market as there would be a lot of ready stock and price may remain stable.

When you approach a seller or builder for a flat/plot/house purchasing, you must remember to check out the following aspects:

1. **Builder's Reputation:** Purchasing a house always means a huge amount of money, which is why you should always look for projects made by reputed builders or companies.,. In case of a listed company, you can easily find information regarding its financial status in the company's balance sheet. If the company is over-leveraged, it is a good idea to avoid

purchasing a property in any of its projects since high debt increases the probability of delay in projects completion.

You should also find out how many projects the developer has delivered in the past. Avoid novices as they usually lack the financial strength to weather a downturn. Visit builder's past projects and find out the truth about builder's reputation. Did the developer hand over the possession on time? Did he provide all the promised on-campus facilities and the specifications in the apartments? How well has he maintained the project after its completion?

How Can You Check The Builder's Reputation?

i. **Market Report & Background of Promoters/ Directors:** Google the company's name and you will find a lot of information about it on blogs, consumer forums, news reports, property sites, etc. Existing customers of the builder who have purchased property from him will provide you exact and true information. At times, you may also see feedback left by customers on the website or blogs. Percentage of appreciation in price is also an indicator of the market report of a builder. The current market price of the builder's past projects in comparison to that of the other projects in the same locality is also an indicator of the builder's standing.

ii. **Financial Position of the Developer's Company:** The banks that either provide the project finance to the developer or approve the builder's project for retail home loans are responsible for checking the financial position of the developer's company. The lender scrutinizes the balance sheet as well as profit and loss account statement of the developer's company. If the company is over leveraged then it will be unable to repay its loan which may cause the project to be delayed. Banks and NBFCs also take the help of the concerned Registrars of Companies office. The Ministry of Corporate Affairs' website (mca.gov.in) is also helpful.

iii. **Real Estate Rating or Grading of Projects:** Most of the times, when a property buyer considers investing in a property, the investment is usually his entire life's savings. Hence, there is an increasing need to distinguish real estate projects on various parameters such as developer's track record, ability to complete project on time, maintaining legal and construction standards, quality of legal documentation, track record of the project's promoters/director. There are some rating agencies which provide an in-depth rating of real estate projects. Some of the well known rating agencies are CRISIL Real Estate Star Ratings, CARE real estate star rating and ICRA real estate star grading. They provide city-specific assessment of real estate projects, and can help you to compare and identify best projects in a particular city. Rating agency only rate those developers, who have registered themselves with rating agency.

iv. **Track Record of The Builder:** It is safer to buy from an experienced developer because he is likely to have a more professional approach, with systems and processes in place. You should check his track record and find out how well the past projects have been executed. Remember, lack of transparency is a good enough reason to not buy. Normally, it is given in advertisement that developer is a member of CREDAI (Confederation of Real Estate Developers Association of India), or BAI (Builder's Association of India). These are self-regulatory bodies that have strict norms for builders and any deviation may lead to the company being blacklisted by the association. So select a builder who must be member of at least one of two above mentioned organizations.

v. **Quality Certificate:** These are issued by certain international organizations. You may use these certificates to check quality of a project before investing in a housing project. The International Organization for Standardization's 9001:2008 certification criteria for a quality management system is based on eight principles, including customer focus and satisfaction. Therefore, an ISO 9001:2008 audited and certified builder is expected to be more professional in his approach.

Always Focus on Construction Quality: All builders boast about their construction quality. A short-cut to evaluating the quality is to go with established, big developers. Basically construction quality depends on the reputation of the builder. Since their reputation for quality construction is their primary ambassador in a competitive market, branded builders employ trusted contractors and ensure proper quality control measures throughout the construction process. They follow standardized construction norms, which do not vary from project to project. They do not allow their contractors to use cheap fittings and accessories. They use branded fittings and offer maintenance contract to reputed facilities management agencies. If one is considering investing in a project by a well-known builder, it makes sense to visit and inspect some of the older projects by the same builder, preferably those that are five to ten years old.

The construction quality of a building can be judged through various parameters, such as its architectural design, the quality of interior design, the brands used for electrical and bathroom fixtures, paints, etc.

Patched up cracks on a building's exterior can also be an indicator that the project has a faulty foundation. Small cracks on the walls, creaking or sticking doors and windows, and improperly aligned or uneven floors also indicators of poor finishing.

The other part of the project, say, walls, is comparatively easy to understand. If the construction quality is strong, you will find it very difficult to hammer a nail in the walls after occupation. Lastly, while hunting for a property, which is under construction make sure that, you look at more than just the sample flat.

You may reject a property on the basis of poor construction, finishing or design. Moreover, as it has been said earlier, you should also evaluate the past projects of the builder to know their construction quality, track record etc. However, what if it is a new builder with his maiden project? In such cases, you need to check if the builder's projects have been approved by a rating company. If not, then you can visit the project with a civil engineer to evaluate the construction quality.

2. **Does the Builder/Developer have any tie-ups with Banks?:** All developers prefer tie-ups with Banks and Non Banking Finance Companies. In this tie-up procedure, builder provides his title papers of property with all approvals obtained from concerning authorities. Bank also scrutinizes the balance sheet of Developer Company as well as that of its directors. Bank panel advocate play an important role for conducting the title search and checking all approvals. Banks also consider the experience of the builder in real estate. Before you finalize a flat, ensure that the project is approved by at least two nationalized banks and two top Housing Finance Companies.

3. **Check The Land Use And Legal Report Of Property:** The term 'land use' means the purpose of the land on which the building is being constructed. Land use may be for residential or commercial purpose. The local development authority issues such type of approvals. Check the property documents whether they have residential construction approvals or if the building is commercial, then ask builder to show you commercial approval or conversion of residential land into commercial land. Next step is to check the titles of property whether builder is owner of the plot on which building is being constructed or he is just a developer of that plot which belongs to another owner and the two of them have signed a land owner–developer agreement.

   Friends, always remember that this agreement should be registered. Normally reputed developers don't show their all title papers to buyers. This is because they have a reputation in the market and they just have to tell the purchasers that their project is approved by so many banks and bank's lawyers and officers have inspected the chain of documents. However if the builder is new or does not have a track record, then ask the developer to show you the paper which proves his ownership of the land. Every plot has a unique khasra number. Ask the builder for that number and check in whose name the plot is registered. You can hire a lawyer to conduct the title search. He can also find out if there is any legal dispute over the land.

4. **Check all Approval Letters from the Concerned Departments:** When any developer starts a project, he has to obtain approvals from many departments and get documents such as the map approval letter from concerned town planning agency/development authority. Also inquire whether the builder has received the other mandatory approvals related to the building plan, pollution, water,

environment and height clearance (if the building is situated within a radius of 25 Km from airport boundary) from the Airport Authority of India.

5. **Has Land Acquisition been Completed?:** Often developers begin to sell apartments before the land acquisition is over. Some unforeseeable problems may arise due to which acquisition may not be completed. The developer may manage to buy 80% of the land he needs but may get embroiled in a dispute over the balance 20%. Now, if that one tower in which your apartment was planned was to be developed on the disputed 20%, you would get into trouble.

6. **Check the Payment Plan of Builder:** The payment plan of the builder also plays an important role in flat purchasing hence you should pay attention to the payment plan. Remember, most developers will levy a penalty if you plan to shift to a construction-linked plan midway. So decide which plan suits you at the very beginning. Remember, once you have paid the entire money, you are at the mercy of the developer if the project is delayed or postponed.

7. **Check if there is any Escalation Clause:** One day, one of the customers of my branch approached me and said that he wanted an additional loan of ₹2 lakh. Our bank had already financed him a loan of ₹20 lakh against price of the flat, which was ₹25 lakh. I asked him the reason for extra loan since the flat was ready for registry. He told me that builder had increased cost of villa to ₹28 lakh against sale consideration of ₹25 lakh due to the wrong measurement of villa size at the time of agreement to sale. Now actual size of villa is more than mentioned size in agreement to sale. He further discussed with me that should he approach a consumer court. I read the agreement and told him that builder had included cost escalation clause in agreement to sale. So, I told him that he had to pay extra cost. Some builders often

include a cost-escalation clause in the agreement to sale which states that if the cost of building materials or other inputs goes up or there is chance of increasing of flat or villa area, the builder reserves the right to hike the cost of the flat. Therefore you should always make enquiries regarding the builder's track record of whether has he implemented escalation clause in the past. Did he have a genuine reason to implement the clause? Moreover, if the area of the flat increases, at what rate will you have to pay the difference? Will it be as per the original booking rate or the current rate? If you do not want to pay the escalation cost, then opt for a developer who does not include an escalation clause in agreement to sale.

8. **Find Out the Date of Completion of Project:** Almost all reputable builders mention the time of possession of flat. Normally a particular month with year is mentioned like, March 2021. Some developers mention that the project will be completed within a certain period, say, 30-36 months from the start of construction (some blocks whose map are approved earlier will be ready for possession earlier than others). They also mention a period of about six month after the completion date of project. Sometimes the project experiences construction delays due to some reasons which are not under the control of the builder. These reasons could include strike of labor, non availability of building materials or labors etc. Always ask builder to mention the date of completion. Also enquire from the builder that if the project delays, what is the amount of the penalty paid to the customer. Try to find out if his earlier project was completed on time and if not, then did he pay any penalty to buyers or did he find a way to circumvent it?

9. **Is There A Penalty Clause?:** Project delays are a reality and very few are completed on schedule time. Some builders do

offer compensation for delays in handing over possession, but it's not something you can bank upon. The penalty amount will be nowhere close to the EMI you are paying. This is because you would be paying the installment for the total cost of property, but the compensation offered will be linked to the base price, which does not include additional charges for parking, club membership, etc. Some builders provide you an amount equal to your proposed monthly income based on the area in which project is situated. Some builders slip a clause in the agreement, which insulates them against any claim by the buyer if the project delays. Others have an upper limit for the compensation that they will pay. Most, however, have a clause in the agreement which states that if the project is delayed because of factors outside their control, they will not be liable.

There have also been cases where cheques issued for these penalty charges have bounced. Getting compensation from the builder is not so easy. Prevention is your best bet.

10. **What Will Be The Size/Area Of Flat Or Villa?:** Remember that the 'area' concept is used varyingly in the real estate. Some builders and sellers take advantage of this ambiguity. The end-buyer must be clear as what he/she will get out of a deal as a potential buyer. A few facts to remember:

   ❖ Super built-up area takes into account all the area under the common spaces, which is the apartment's proportionate share of the lobby, staircase, elevator and the corridor outside the apartment. Areas under common facilities like basement, sub-stations, security room, garbage chutes are also included. Moreover, in some cases even window projections and area under stilt is also sometimes included in the super built up area calculations.

- Built-up area is inclusive of not just the carpet area but also the area occupied by the walls of your house.
- Carpet area is defined as the precise area within the walls of your home. If you had to lay out a wall-to-wall carpet in your entire home, they are covered would be the carpet area.

One can easily realize the importance of understanding how each square foot (sq ft) calculated in a particular deal can directly translate into significant amounts that need to be spent purchasing the property. After REREA implementation builder can deal only in carpet area concept.

11. **Do You Get The Same Flat What You Have Seen?:** When you visit the site where project is being constructed the sales person of company will show you a sample flat. Basically, sample flat is marketing tool to attract customers so that company can increase its sale. The interior designers hired by the builders to make the sample flats are experts at creating optical illusions. They know how to use the effects of lighting and place furniture in such a way that the house appears bigger. They use the furniture which is smaller in size than that available in market so customer feels that there will be sufficient space in the flat after the placement of the double bed and other furniture. The sample flats are demolished immediately after the flats are sold out or building is ready for possession. There is also an issue related to location of flat. Sample flats are stand-alone units that offer a great view from every balcony and window. It may not be so when it is a part of a cluster of flats. Some builders often slip in a clause stating that they can alter the layout plan of the flat or apartment that was shown to you. Hence, the final flat layout may be quite different from the sample flat that you saw at the time of booking. The sample flat can appear to be much larger

than the real one. For a buyer, a better indicator of what he will get is the architectural drawing of the apartment, as well as the layout map of the project, which is approved by Municipal Corporation or local development authority. These drawings will tell you the exact carpet area of the flat. Friends, please remember you will not be able to drag the builder to consumer court if the agreement contains a clause stating that the builder can change the specifications.

Some builders show you the layout plan of a building at the time of booking which has a garden and swimming pool/ club house and situated close to the apartment you may buy. However, later in the construction phase you discover that the block in which you have booked your flat is not close to a garden but another foundation of another block of township. It means builder altered the construction plan midway. Friends, ideally the builder should construct the building as per the approved map. He cannot change the plan which has been approved. However, at the time of booking, the sales persons generally show you a brochure which has a more attractive layout plan which differs from the original plan which was approved by the development authority. This is done to lure you into booking the flat. Here you need to know that the area of the flat cannot be increased.

12. **Is An Early Exit Permitted?:** Many people buy flats for investment purposes and you may also be one of them. If you are getting a high return before the completion of project, as an investor you may prefer to sell your flat to another buyer. Sometimes, due to some personal reasons, you may not want to keep the flat and may want to sell it. So friends, before signing an agreement to sale, ask the builder whether an early exit is permitted or not. When a builder owns the inventory, he will not be interested to cancel the

flat. Normally, the builder may have a transfer clause in which they charge a fee according to size of flat which may be ₹25/square feet. They normally impose curbs so that people are not able to buy from the secondary market. So you need to investigate if the developer has blocked such sales in the past and the amount of transfer fee that was charged for an early exit?

13. **Can You Get a Refund If You Cancel The Flat?:** Getting a refund from a cash-strapped builder is not easy. Remember, prevention is better than cure and hence if you want to avoid getting into a situation where you need to ask for a refund from the builder, you need to do your homework well, before you book a flat. Cancellation fee greatly varies from developer to developer. Some reputed builders like, Ashiana return the entire money if the buyer cancels the purchase within a month. Some builders don't deduct any money within a month, other deduct 10% of the booking amount, while others quote the same figure on the purchase price of the flat and some smaller developers may forfeit the entire booking amount. Hence, there are no clear norms that the builders are required to follow while cancelling bookings.

    Think twice before you give the cheque or the cash. Even after you have decided on a project, avoid paying the booking amount in cash. Friends, always have a cheque book with you while finalizing a flat and issue the cheque in favor of developer. Always obtain receipt of cheque given to builder.

14. **What Are The Extra Charges?:** Extra charges include parking (open or cover). Cover parking charges are more as compared to open parking.

    If you are interested to buy a house that has a corner location overlooking hills on one side and a central garden on the other. Now both these preferences will come with a price tag. There is always a price differential even between different properties within the same complex or even the same building depending on the floor, the view, the size and other factors.

East or south-facing properties fetch better values than north and west-facing properties, especially in north India, where winters are very cold and summers very hot. If your house faces east or south, you are likely to get more sunshine during the winter. Similarly, in South India, vastu-compliant units have a premium on them.

Users in metro cities pay more for a view. In Mumbai, for instance, the price per unit rises as you go to a higher floor. This is true of any water-facing city where the view of the water is considered a premium. The higher you go, the better the sea view. If the property is sea-facing, there is a hefty extra sum that the buyer has to shell out. Elsewhere, in high-rise apartments, the units facing the central courtyard are priced higher than those that face another apartment. Pool or park-facing properties also have a higher value. Sometimes road-facing properties are charged a premium.

In cities (like Jaipur) that are not quite used to high-rises yet, the premium is for the ground to sixth floor. Here, the consumer still clings to old-city values of living in low-rises while simultaneously availing of the safety, security and convenience that high-rises offer. As a result, they look for lower floors in high-rise building. Higher floors do not command a premium vis-a-vis lower floors in such cases.

If your new flat faces a garden or a swimming pool, then you may have to pay some extra charges, which are usually calculated per square feet. Such charges are known as preferential location charges (PLCs). The concept of Preferred Location Charges (PLC) for new properties is based on these principles. Whatever is most in demand is considered premium and charged a PLC. Currently, PLC is arbitrary and there are no fixed norms for it.

You will also need to pay external and internal development charges to the developer. Checkout the amounts and also find out if they are subject to change. Inquire from the builder if there are any other charges. The decision to book a flat should only be taken after understanding and considering all charges. You should only purchase a flat if the total amount after bargaining is within your budget.

15. **What If You Don't Pay On Time?:** Normally builders provide a grace period for paying up any missed installments. However, you need to inquire about the amount of grace time allowed by the builder to make the payment in case of any unforeseen delays in the payment of the installments. Also inquire about your interest liability. Normally builders charge the interest at the rate of 18% per annum. In case of delayed payments, inquire if your allotment will be cancelled? Also inquire about the provisions of the forfeiture clause? Also, in case of forfeiture, what is the amount of the refund that will be issued? Remember, if your payments are late or if you miss an installment, you can be liable for a specified penalty.

16. **Is The Property Mortgaged?:** Ask the builder if he has a project loan. Then, you must obtain a NOC from the bank from which builder has taken the project loan. Banks also issue a demand draft mentioning the escrow account number (account of the bank in which sale proceeds of a particular project are to be deposited) of the builder. Also obtain permission to mortgage from builder. Unless you do this, you will not be able to get the property registered in your name.

17. **These Rates Will Be Revised Soon!:** In this era of cut throat competition, every builder wants to increase his sale so this trick is often used by builders to entice buyers. If you tell a builder that you need time to think it over or visit it again with other family members, he may say that the project is almost sold out and prices will soon be revised and will be increased..

    The truth is that today's real estate market is a buyers' market. Developers are more desperate to sell as compared to the buyers' eagerness to purchase. Overheated markets, sliding stock prices and rising interest rates have made matters worse. Bank's norms for builder's finance are tight so the money is not cheap for builders. The cheapest form of money for developers is the sale proceeds of flats received from buyers. If builders think that you are a serious buyer, then they will be ready for negotiation and also provide you the discount.

    If you are not planning to buy a house now, the best strategy is to be a pretend buyer and save for your dream house. If you keep putting away the EMI amount in a safe investment option, you will be able to save for a higher down payment when you eventually take the plunge.

18. **Don't Be Lured By Freebies:** When you are hunting for a property, a range of price discounts and special offers are offered by builders to expedite sales. Different developers make different types of offers. Some offer free trips to a foreign country and others a luxury car. Some offer a free modular kitchen with AC in bedrooms or free parking and some others may waive preferential location charge.

    Friends, keep in mind that no one can offer things from his pocket. So always keep your focus on the flat that you are buying. What's the area of the flat? What's the per square feet rate at which the developer is offering the apartment? Is it at par with the rates prevailing in the market? You can calculate the exact monetary value of the freebies, deduct it from the base price, and then compare it with the other offers. You should consider the financial background of the builder before opting for these schemes.

What to Look out for as an End User?

If you are buying for self-use, it has to be where you would like to stay in the long term. Property is not a very liquid asset and it is important for you to be able to stay in the house you bought for at least a few years. The profile of other buyers and the neighborhood, facilities and amenities that come with it, future infrastructure projects in the area, transport connectivity and state of roads are all issues you would want to find out before you buy.

Now assess which locality is convenient from a travel time perspective. Sometimes you may find a property that you like but it may be too far from your place of work or the people you want to stay close to make a rational choice between affordability, the type of property and the conveniences in the locality. You have a choice between new, first-sale property, second sale of new property and just buying older property.

When you buy a property from the developer at launch, there are certain inaugural discounts you can avail. If you buy from brokers at the time of launch, they also pass on some part of the brokerage to you via a credit note. This amount is paid to you when the developer pays the broker his commission (generally after a few installments).

When you buy a newly constructed property at any stage before possession, you are entering the secondary market as a buyer. These properties are normally sold by the previous buyer who entered the buying cycle at a lower rate and is booking profits and selling to another buyer. When the market cycles are good and the property market buoyant, there may be several sales during the life cycle of the construction of the apartment.

You can search for the current value of the property on various websites by specifying the required configuration. Once you get several options, compare facilities, prices and listings. These may be posted by either individuals or agents. You may choose to use the services of agents or deal directly with individual sellers. If an agent is representing a seller, then the brokerage is paid by the seller.

The value of the property rises as it reaches the possession stage. Each of these factors affects the quality of your stay and also determines the price that you have to pay. If you are buying for future use, you should be able to compute the profile of the neighborhoods into the future. A good way to begin is to create three categories:

- Transport infrastructure-expressways, flyovers public transport, metro, suburban rail links and distances from airport and railway station.
- Physical infrastructure water, power, sewerage, drainage and roads.
- Social infrastructure-schools, colleges, hospitals, retail facilities, entertainment options and sports facilities.

Should you Invest in Small Cities

When investing in smaller cities, you need to do meticulous local market research. Use information available in news papers and online on magicbricks.com, 99acres.com, OLX Homes etc. to understand the types of property there and how prices have moved over a period of time. You should also participate in online forums were buyers talk to each other about the projects available. You may also take help from local property dealers. There is a strong possibility that the developers in small cities may be local builders with whom you are not familiar. It is best to check the antecedents of the developer and also try and talk to others who have bought from the group. The reputation of the builder and the quality of construction are very important when you want to exit your investment.

Should you Invest in Periphery and Suburbs of Big Cities

Advantages of Investing in Suburbs of Big Cities There are two types of people who prefer to buy in the suburbs-those looking for spacious luxury or those who look for places that are affordable. Both are possible because suburbs are often less expensive than downtown or city areas. For those moving to the suburbs, spacious luxury, and proximity to the metro city, affordable property prices, quality infrastructure and availability of well-managed residential spaces are the key factors.

Common Mistakes to Avoid before Buying a Property

1. Do not buy into a township because a friend or colleague bought there. Understand where you want to live as an end-user. This includes the location near your friends and family, close to places you often visit, a neighborhood in which you would be comfortable, etc. Your relatives or friends may not live where your friend's relatives or friends stay.

2. Do not go for any development or developer by hearsay. Check out the location, the sample flat or even earlier developments by the developer. If there are seepages, weak maintenance or bad parking issues, avoid that development.
3. Do not assume that just because a property is in your budget, it is the right one for you. While affordability is very important, it is also important to make a checklist of

features that are important to you, e.g., safety, east or south facing, view, location, distance from entertainment or retail or commercial hubs.

4. Do not buy without enquiring what kind of people are buying there. The profile of your neighbor is something that you have to live with for a long time. Even if you have friends and family close by, your neighbors and their profiles are very important for living comfort.
5. Do not buy without checking basic amenities such as water, power and their back-ups, clubs and swimming pools and sports facilities if you are an outdoors person and car parking facilities to house your vehicles. These can become major irritants when you start staying in the development.
6. Do not buy into facilities that you don't need. You will end up paying for these in the long-term but may never use them. For instance, if you are riot spotty at a sports club membership may be of no use to you. If you have bought into a golf links apartments, you don't need a golf course membership unless you are a player. If you take on services that you are unlikely to use, there will be regular payments of maintenance charges and your cost of living will go up unnecessarily.
7. Don't buy a house adjacent to school, marriage garden or hospital because sometimes it may create nuisance.

❑

18

Property Purchasing Plans Offered by Developers

In the real estate sector, competition is increasing day-by-day and the sales are slowing down. Due to these factors, developers are coming up with a variety of attractive offers to persuade customers to buy.

Here's What you should know before Opting for these Plans

Down Payment Plan

This is a plan where buyer has to pay the entire money (the amount stated in the agreement) to the builder/developer at the time of booking of the flat/villa. Normally in this type of booking, buyer has to pay 10% amount at the time of booking. 80 to 85% amount has to be deposited within one month from the date of booking.

In case of any delays in the project, the customer's money might be stuck indefinitely. This plan should only be selected when builder has a great reputation and the customer uses his savings to pay the amount (bank loan is not possible in this type of scheme). In September 2013, RBI has instructed the banks to refrain from offering a home loan which has such a payment plan.

Time Linked Plan

This is a plan where purchaser has to pay amount as per scheduled time mentioned in allotment letter issued by builder/developer. This plan is normally offered by Government Organizations (National Building Construction Corporation Limited, Housing Boards of State Governments). The allottee has to pay the money as per the mentioned dates. The apartment is offered on a reasonable price. This plan is offered by government organizations, so the possession of flats is generally given within the scheduled timeline.

Flexi-Payment Plan

In this plan the purchaser has to pay 10% of money (agreement amount) to builder/developer at the time of booking the flat/villa. 30-40% amount is paid within the next one month. The rest of the amount is to be paid as per the construction stage of the building/project. Purchaser generally gets 6 to 8% discount.

Construction Linked Plan

This is a plan where buyer has to pay 10% of money (agreement amount) to builder/developer at the time of booking of the flat/villa. 10% of the amount has to be paid within the next one month and the rest of the amount is paid in accordance to the construction stage of the building/project. Normally, the builder demands 10% on the roof casting of each floor. Purchaser gets about 2 to 3 years for payments.

Benefits

This is a good scheme since payments are linked to the stages of completion of the construction. In this, there are a lot of benefits in case the purchaser opts for a home loan. During the construction phase, he only has to pay the interest amount of the disbursed loan amount and may also save some amount as margin money.

This scheme is relatively less risky since the entire amount is not invested right away and the builder gets the money in stages.

Drawbacks

While this plan appears attractive, builders have found a way to circumvent it for their own benefit. By the time the superstructure (skeleton) is ready, the buyer or his bank has paid 80-90% of the apartment's cost. The next stage, in which the interior and finishing (doors, windows and marble fittings) is done generally, takes between six months to one year.

However, instead of finishing up the project, the builder at the beginning of the finishing stage, begins to delay the project, stretching it from two to four years. Having collected most of the apartment's cost, he now diverts the buyer's funds to his other projects or to buy land for next project. This causes the buyers money to get stuck which makes them feel cheated.

Possession Linked Plan

It is the latest payment plan which has been inspired by the current slow down and helps reduce the risk of delays in the delivery of the final product (home). Now-a-days, most of the developers who are financially sound are opting for possession linked plans (PLP) rather than construction linked plans (CLP).

Benefits

Under the PLP plan, the payment is made in two stages. While 10-25% of the total cost is paid at the time of booking/within a month, the balance is payable after the buyer has received the property's possession. The plan's biggest advantage is that it reduces the development risk (the risk that the project may be delayed or not be developed at all) for the buyer). Under this plan, the builder has to take responsibility to complete the project on schedule so that he can collect the balance money from the buyer. Since the buyer has paid only 10-25% of the total cost, he has lesser amount at stake as compared to CLP.

This plan also offers monetary benefits. With 20-25% of the total cost in your pocket, you can book an apartment. Thereafter, you get two-three years—the time it takes to develop the project—to accumulate more money. This means that you don't have to take a large loan. Under the CLP, the buyer takes the home loan at the time of booking. During the construction period, he has to bear the burden of the pre-EMI (the interest component on the loan) as well as the rent. With the PLP plan, he saves on the pre-EMI cost entirely.

Watch out for... ....

While the PLP plan is an improvement over the CLP, home buyers should look closely at a few things before opting for it.

1. **Difference In The Costs:** Is the cost under PLP the same as under CLP? The total cost of the flat/villa should be the same under both PLP and CLP plans. If the price is different for the two, then the developer has already included the cost of funding in the PLP plan. It means he will collect interest from you and pass up the offer to you.

Builders usually build in a 10-15% premium over standard rates while offering the PLP scheme. Bargaining hard on the apartment's price may not be possible when you opt for such a scheme.

2. **Check The Builder's Financial Strength:** Under the PLP scheme, a higher proportion of the risk is transferred to the developer. Hence, the buyer should ensure that the developer has the financial strength to complete the project and has received funding from a bank.

3. **Due Diligence of Property/Builder:** The due diligence associated with the purchase of a flat should not be overlooked. Are all the approvals for developing the project in place? How good is the developer's track record regarding timely completion of projects? Does the location justify the cost? What will be the carpet area of the apartment as opposed to its super built-up area? Also, make sure that the developer has not cut down on the quality of facilities and specifications to reduce costs. Also try to find out whether project is approved by at least two public sector banks.

Should You Go For The Pure PLP Plan?

YES!

This means that there should only be two payments, one at the time of booking and the other on possession. The developers' need for cash is so high that they will offer you all sorts of enticements. One way in which developers are trying to circumvent the ban on the 80:20 schemes is that the buyer opts for the CLP plan and takes a loan from the bank. The developer pays the interest on the loan till possession to the buyer and the latter pays the money to the bank. Such agreements with the developer are fraught with risk. What if he does not pay you the interest? If you default on the bank loan, the liability is entirely yours.

Finally, the PLP plan is the result of the slowdown in the industry and developers' need to push sales. It may not be offered once the market picks up, so make the most of it while it is available.

❑

19

Pre-launch Booking

What is Pre-Launching?

It is a situation where a builder declares to start/launch a project in a new place. At this time, he does not have the approved map or any official permission. In this stage the developer only informs an inner circle of his old clients, brokers, investors, friends and relatives of the availability of properties in a project that has not been officially introduced in the market. The builder will ask the buyer to deposit a post dated cheque and will give him a receipt of the cheque. However, at this stage this only an oral agreement and nothing has been documented so far. The news of the new project spreads by the word of mouth and even email but does not figure on the developer's website or in any other marketing media. The buyers who show interest on pre-launch projects are usually investors and end-users who seek to benefit from the price advantage and can wait for a couple of years before getting possession. At this time there is a board on project site mentioned "XYZ Project of ABC company ltd is coming soon". In this situation, buyers directly contact the builder or Real Estate Company to book the flat/villa.

The basic-purpose of pre-launching is that the developer can gauge the response of the public for his new/upcoming project. It helps him to understand the viability of the project. If there are lots of bookings, he can decide to proceed further otherwise postpone the projects completely or for the time being. They may also get interest-free capital from the market by pre-launching their projects. This capital can be used by them as margin money if they want a project loan.

Is It Technically Right?

No! Technically, it is wrong because developer can only take bookings in a project after obtaining all legal and technical approvals/ permissions from competent authorities.

Benefits for Buyer:

- The price advantage of buying a property at the pre-launch stage can be 5 to 10 per cent, depending on various market factors.
- During the pre-launch phase, the buyer contacts builder directly so he can save brokerage.
- It is the best for an investor who only books flats to make profit and sells them after taking advantage of price appreciation.

Drawbacks:

- It is technically wrong.
- There is lack of clarity about flat number and floor on which you would be allotted the flat.
- Sometimes due to the poor response in the pre-launch phase, the builder finds it difficult to start a project. However, in the mean time he may have used the booking money in other projects so he may take time to refund the money. If the developer does not have a good reputation, your booking money may be on stake.

- Investing in pre-launched projects is a high-risk undertaking, which can pay off as long as one has factored in all possible variables. It makes most sense to investors who have a high risk appetite and the ability to weather an eventual setback. Investing in pre-launches is, generally speaking, not a route that end-users are advised to take, unless there is a high degree of certainty implied in the builder's brand and track record. So, the whole picture depends on the developer's reputation. However, buyers must keep in mind that the project might not have got all required approvals or might not be cleared for home loan approvals by lenders. Another risk is that the project could be delayed or even shelved if the developer is not able to raise enough money.

What are the precautions to be kept in mind before opting for Pre-Launch Booking?

Although pre-launch booking is distinctly cheaper, but it involves a great amount of risk. So, before investing in a pre-launch booking, you must check the following points.

1. Always choose a well-known and an established builder.
2. You should know whether the builder has free and clear ownership of the land on which the project is being built.
3. Always make payments via demand draft or post dated cheque so that incase of dispute you can take legal help.
4. Always inquire about the area in which project is to be launched. You should find out if there is any real estate activity in that particular area or it only has new government projects.
5. Check out whether the land on which project is to be launched is away from the airport boundary or not close to any army area.

6. Check if all the approvals and title papers are in place.
7. It is necessary to investigate the builder's record on transparent dealings and compliance with legal formalities, overall record for timely project completion and the experience he has.
8. The project must have a commencement certificate in place. So friends, only book in the pre-launch phase after studying all pros and cons of project.

Note: Pre-Launch Booing is prohibited in RERA.

❑

20

Consider your Family Size before Finalizing a Property

Some years back, Mr. Vishnu Chauhan who was working in leading Real Estate Company approached me for a home loan to purchase a two BHK flat in a project which was under development. At the time, he was a bachelor. Loan was sanctioned.

Last year, he again approached the bank and told the branch manager that he wanted to replace the property in loan. He had changed his mind and wanted to purchase a three BHK flat instead of already purchased two BHK flat in the same under construction apartment. He further told the branch manager that he would bear extra cost of flat size and did not want to increase the loan amount.

Since Vishnu is a good friend. I asked him the reason for his decision. He told me that now he was married and had two children. His parents would also like to live with him so he required more space than earlier. Dear friends, Mr. Vishnu's case may be considered as one of those unique cases where the bank relented since the apartment was under construction and Mr. Vishnu was company's employee However, these kinds of changes are not possible for everyone every time. Hence, it is better to make a long term plan when making such decisions.

The size of the family or the number of family members living with us keeps varying with time and in different stages of life. Let us take the example of Mr. Yogesh. In 2005, he was a bachelor. He got married in 2006. In the next five years, his family size increased from two members to four members.

Newly married couples often suffer due to this oversight. They purchase a studio flat or a one BHK flat little realizing that later when they have children and their old parents living with them, they will need more rooms. When the children grow up, they may need separate study rooms too.

So friends, if you are thinking of buying or are already in the process of buying a dream home which may be a budget home or a big home or a luxurious flat or a villa or a farm house, do some simple calculations. Calculate the size of your family, how many children do you have or expected or desired number of children in the years to come. You should also account for many other dependents (parents, unmarried sister or any other) will be living with you in the years to come. The answers to these questions will help you in making the right decision.

❑

21

Should you Purchase a Property if the seller has Lost the Title Papers?

One day my friend Mohit came to my office with photocopies of some documents and told me that he wanted to purchase a plot and construct a house on it. Since I know him very well and am familiar with his income, I replied in the positive. When I was processing the loan, I asked him to call the seller for the original documents of the property. He told me that the seller had lost the original papers and had only certified copies, news papers cutting showing missing property documents with a receipt of FIR reported in police station. He also told me that he had given ₹10 lakh as an advance. Being a banker, as well as a good friend I was shocked. I discussed the case with my panel advocate and senior officials and after that I denied the home loan.

Friends, always ask the seller to show original documents of property before closing the deal and avoid purchasing a property where seller has lost the chain of documents fully or partially.

Why?

Normally, banks and housing finance companies are reluctant to providing loans to buyers if the original property documents are missing. This is because there may be a possibility that the owner has mortgaged the house/plot/flat and the original documents are with the bank. In case he vanishes the purchaser will not only lose money but may also be saddled with a loan. The seller may be a cheater who has already sold the property and is residing in the sold property as a tenant and just pretending to be the owner. People can cheat you in numerous ways in case the original documents are missing. Inspecting and checking the paperwork and the credentials of the property and its owner in the absence of the original documents can be a cumbersome and costly affair.

But there may be some cases where you can take a decision to purchase a property which does not have the original title.

- Seller is well known to you or your close friend or a trust worthy relative.
- If only one or two papers are missing which doesn't affect title of ownership.

However before taking any decision you should approach a bank for loan. The decision to lend money in such situations is decided on a case-to-case basis. Usually, the result will be more favorable if both the purchaser/borrower and seller know each other, as well as both have enjoyed a long- term relationship with the bank. After considering application, bank official will conduct additional inspection of property. The bank's panel advocate will first verify all the documents associated with the property, including the police complaint records. Then he will check whether all duplicate documents are genuine and not forged. Bank will also conduct the inspection of the seller with due diligence as well as ask him to complete KYC.

If your deal involves a large amount of money, then publish the details of the property in two news papers, one local and other national, stating that you are going to purchase the said property and also add that if someone has any objection, they can contact you / raise the objection within 30 days. The bank may also ask both the seller and the buyer to give separate undertakings that if and when the original documents are found; they would be handed over to the bank. If the bank finds the above mentioned formalities satisfactory, it may offer the loan. All the expenses related to these activities are generally borne by the borrower.

Keeping the Documents Safe

As a house owner you should be careful while storing the property documents. The best option is to take a bank loan so that the safe keeping of the documents safe will be responsibility of the bank. If you have not taken home loan then you may apply for a bank locker for safekeeping these property documents. But after these all precautions, property papers may still get lost while travelling or any other mishap. Misplacing original documents doesn't mean that you cannot sell or buy a property. While you can settle the deal in such a case, it will require additional paperwork and result in higher costs.

How to Get Duplicate Documents?

When you lose such important documents, the first step is to file an FIR in police station stating that the documents have been lost, misplaced or stolen, and get a copy of the complaint. Normally bank keeps property documents in safe custody but in rare cases due to negligence of the bank officers, the documents may be misplaced by the bank. In this case, the FIR will have to be filed by the bank. Buyers should ask for a copy of the FIR from the seller.

You will also have to place an advertisement, stating the loss of the documents, in an English daily newspaper, as well as a regional one. Buyer of the property can also place such an advertisement and, through it, call for any claimant to the property within 15 days of the advertisement being published.

Property documents may include lease deed issued by a development authority, sale deed which is registered in sub registrar. Friends, steps to be taken are different in each case.

In case of a property being a flat, based on the police complaint, the owner can apply for a duplicate share certificate from the housing society, which can put up the application at its meeting. If the application is approved, the housing society will issue a copy of the share certificate after charging a fee. Another document that owners and buyers need from the housing society is the no-objection certificate, without which no lender will be willing to provide a loan. So, ensure you get this too.

In case of an individual plot /house, you can only get certified copies of sale deeds. These can be obtained from the registrar's office as since the office maintains the records of all transactions in its jurisdiction. However, the development authorities may issue duplicate title deed/lease, but the deed will be in the name of the first allottee only. For this you have to give an undertaking on a stamp paper, stating that you have lost your original documents. The undertaking should outline the details of the property, the text of advertisement published in the newspaper, and the police complaint number. It should also clearly state that all the details declared in the undertaking are true. This document should then be attested, notarized and registered with a notary. You have to submit copies of the police complaint, the newspaper advertisement, and the undertaking; only then the development authority may issue duplicate copy of title deed. Since the deputy registrar's office has all the details of the property, you can easily get the certified copies of sale deeds from the office. The duplicate documents can cost you anything from ₹10000 to ₹25000.

❑

22

Should you Purchase a Property as a Legacy for Children?

For parents with money to spare, leaving a legacy in the form of property is a personal decision, but it may not be the most practical way to pass on your inheritance to the children. Parent's lives should not be driven by children's needs/desires. If this means not being able to leave behind a property for kids, they should not feel guilty about it.

Property Related Disputes

Approximate 65 % of all civil cases in India are related to property disputes, while 20-25% of all cases decided by the Supreme Court are concerned with land disputes. So, if you buy a property for adult children but die without a will, the property may lead to problems among siblings, more so if a single house is to be split among two or more children. Even with a will, there are likely to be disputes after your death because a will can be contested easily. Besides, archaic property laws mean that the judicial resolution might take several years and your children may end up spending a lot of money.

Property for Personal Use

If your children are living abroad or in different cities within the country, they may not need the house for personal use. If they do decide to retain it after retirement, it will either require major renovation or will need to be sold in exchange for a new one. This will require a lot of money and physical presence, besides turning into a tedious and cumbersome process for children staying in far off places.

Investment in Property

If the property is to be used as an investment by adult children, don't pass it on through a will. To avoid disputes, sell it during your lifetime and distribute the money among them. If you do want to leave a legacy, you might as well give liquid assets which are easier to transact.

Reverse Mortgage Loan is a Good Choice

This topic will be discussed in detail within the chapter of 'Reverse Mortgage '. If you have bought property as a legacy for kids, but the latter do not need it or you run short of funds in retirement, reverse mortgage is an option. This will help generate additional income while you are alive, and offer a good way of selling the property after you die. This is because the lending institution will dispose it off after your death without the children's intervention. If kids want to keep the property, they will need enough funds to repay the loan.

❑

23

How to Purchase a Low Budget Property?

Some of us have a low budget for buying a property due to so many reasons. But need not worry still you have four options in case you want to purchase a low-budget property.

1. **Investment in a New Project:** You may book a flat in pre-launch period or at the beginning of a new project. The price of the property in these stages is generally low.
2. **Search Resale Property:** Look for old properties that have low resale value.
3. **Purchase Property Outside the City:** If you have a low budget, then purchase a property which is currently on the outskirts of the city. With time as the city grows, the value of the property will appreciate substantially.
4. **Purchase A Property In Bank Auction:** Purchasing a property in an auction is not a common practice. Banks auction those houses (after taking possession) whose owners are not able to repay loans. What makes them attractive is that their selling price is usually advertised as being 15-20% less than the prevailing market price in that particular

locality. However, before you jump at the prospect of buying one, consider the option carefully.

A bank auctions the properties for which the owner is unable to repay the home loan or any other loan for which borrower has mortgaged house as collateral security. If he continues to default for more than 90 days then the bank issues a notice under SARFAESI Act and borrower is asked to deposit the overdue amount within 60 days. If borrower fails to deposit money in the stipulated time, then the property is put up for auction and this is advertised in newspapers.

The bank is only interested in recovering its outstanding principal along with some interest component and the expenses that occurred due to the legal possession of the house. Hence this amount is calculated and listed as the reserve price for the auction. This is usually much lower than the market price of the property. If the final auction price is higher than the reserve price, the extra amount is handed over to the original owner.

What to check before participating in an auction?

The low reserve price may seem tempting, but you need to ascertain whether the amount mentioned by the bank is the gross price or if there are any additional costs that you may have to pay later.

Following are some questions you need to ask before you bid.

Are there any unpaid dues?

When a bank auctions a property, it is sold on an 'as is where is' basis, so you should read the bid document carefully to find out if there are any unpaid dues. The bid document is like the prospectus of an IPO, where all the facts covering the legal title and responsibility for pending dues are stated.

In most cases, the owner is not in a position to pay the dues to the bank and knows that the property will be seized. So he doesn't bother to pay the associated fees, such as the society maintenance charge or lease money /property tax. From the time he receives the first notice till the property is taken over; there is a minimum period of six months. It means that if you buy the house, you will probably have to pay at least six months worth of outstanding dues.

Obviously, the utility bills may not have been paid. It's possible that some utilities may have been disconnected or discontinued; such as the removal of the electricity meter or water connection. So, you will have to pay for renewing the connections, along with the late fee, if any.

How much Repair Work is Needed?

Most banks do little to keep the property in good condition after taking possession. So, you may have to undertake some renovation or maintenance work to make it more habitable. It would be a good idea to visit the property and calculate how extensive the repair work is likely to be and how much it will cost. Also, as the property is being sold on 'as is where is' basis, you will be responsible for any damages that may have been caused directly or indirectly to other properties around it. For instance, if there is water seepage while the house is in the bank's possession and this damages an adjoining property or the one below it, you, as the new owner, will have to pay for it.

It's also possible that the previous owner has left some stuff in the house. You will have to check with the bank about the person who will assume responsibility for it. Will you have to pay extra for any furnishing, furniture or appliances that have been installed by the previous owner? Will the previous owner collect these or will you need to dispose of these? Who will be entitled to the money received on the sale of these items?

Typically, the bank will decide about it after considering the outstanding amount. The ownership of the contents of the property is usually mentioned in the bid document. However, it doesn't hurt to have clarification to avoid any unpleasantness in the future if the previous owner lands at your door to claim his items.

How much will you have to pay immediately after the bid?

Banks fix a higher down payment for the house that is to be auctioned. This is usually 20-25% of the selling price and has to be paid immediately after you place a successful bid. Though a bank has no rule about where you source your home loan, it could help you haggle for the lower end of the down payment range or get a better interest rate if you take it from the same bank. Normally banks provide seven days for arrangement of the remaining amount (which is usually 75-80%) so you should ensure that you research well on the loan front before bidding.

Advantages

If the final price (after taking into account all the additional costs) is lower than the market price, you have obviously landed a good deal. However, you shouldn't mind even if you have to pay a bit more. This is because you can be sure the property is a safe bet as the bank would have checked all the documents thoroughly.

The biggest advantage is that if you purchase a property in bank auction, the sale deed will be executed on full amount so you need not worry paying black money or convert your white money to black money. So in all probability you would be able to get more loans. Besides, you will probably get a house in an established residential location.

❑

24

Different Taxes on Real Estate that affect your Budget

GST (Goods and Service Tax)

The 2017-18 budget imposed GST.

Now, according to the GST Act, the developer or builder of an under-construction property has to pay GST when he sells a property to a buyer. Normally builders pass on this tax liability to buyers of property.

Therefore, although paying GST is mandatory, it can be avoided if

A. The builder has obtained a completion certificate from the issuing authority.

B. If you are constructing a single residential unit.

C. Affordable Housing Scheme.

As per the new rules, GST will be calculated at the rate of 12.00 percent of the gross value/Total purchase price of the property. GST rate will be 5% if builder has opted composite scheme.

TDS on Property

In the Finance Bill 2013 there was an introduction of **Section 194-IA** related to Tax Deduction at Source on Property transfers.

According to the **Finance Bill 2013**, all sale transactions related to transfer of any immovable property, with the consideration amount exceeding ₹50 lakh demands a TDS of about 1 per cent of the transaction amount by the transferee (buyer) at the time of credit or at the time of payment through all mediums.

The tax deducted shall be deposited into the Government Account through any of the authorized bank branches using **eTax** payment option through **NSDL**.

- A person deducting TDS on Property is not mandatorily required to possess a PAN No.
- This provision is applicable to all those transactions effected on or after June 1, 2013.
- Tax deduction at source on transfer of any immovable property exempts rural agricultural lands.

When does TDS on Property come in to the scene?

Transactions of immovable property are usually undervalued and under reported. Thus, in order to improve the reporting mechanism of such transactions, Finance Minster had introduced section 194IA demanding a TDS on property at a rate of 1 per cent when the properties transfer value exceeds ₹50 lakh applicable from 1st June 2013.

Who is liable for TDS during property transactions?

The buyer of the property is responsible for the Tax deduction of about 1 per cent on the transaction amount. Example, if A buys a property worth ₹50 lakh from B, then A is liable for a TDS deduction of 1 per cent (Rs 50,000) and responsible to deposit the same.

What is the procedure if buyer take home loan from Bank?

In this situation buyer/customer/borrower may instruct bank to deduct 1% TDS of total sale consideration from loan amount and ask to deposit the same with government by them directly.

What are required documents from buyer and seller?

Transaction details, basic information of the buyer and seller, the buyer is required to furnish the copies of PAN of both buyer and seller at the time of filling the Form 26QB.

Form 26QB along with the bank challan is required for depositing TDS through offline method at authorized bank branches.

What is the Procedure to be followed?

The TDS amount deducted by the buyer at the time of making payment to the seller has to be deposited within a period of 1 week from the end of the month in which the deduction has been made.

First, the buyer is required to duly fill the form 26QB furnishing all the required details regarding the property purchased, TDS on property calculation under Section 194IA, details of the buyer and seller etc.

Following the form 26QB, the buyer is asked for the preference of depositing TDS on property.

Online

Once, the buyer opts for the online payment procedure, the Form 26QB is automatically redirected to the buyer's e-payment gateway followed by procedures respective to buyer's choice.

Offline

Alternatively, the buyer can opt for an offline mode of payment by taking a print of the duly filled form and submitting the same along with the TDS amount at the authorized bank branches.

After successful submission of the Form 26QB along with the TDS amount, the buyer is required to issue the Form 16B (Certification of TDS under 194IA procured from Centralized Processing Cell of TDS (CPC-TDS) to the seller of the property with respect to the TDS deducted.

❑

25

Bargaining in Real Estate

Now-a-days, in case of real estate, supply is more than the demand. Hence, there are possibilities of bargaining while purchasing a new property. But before purchasing a property, you should do your homework and find out the following facts:-

- What are the rates in that area where you are going to purchase a property?
- What is the market reputation of the builder?
- Since how many years has the company been dealing in real estate?
- What are the facilities available in that particular area? What is the rate of pre-launching a project?
- Why is the builder selling the flats at a higher rate? Find out the factors in the project which may responsible for price appreciation.

More bargaining creates more chances of cheap dealing but you should keep in mind the negative things attached with property so that it may help in bargaining.

Normally, most of the builders are ready to decrease their property prices up to a certain level but they do not declare it officially.

Factors which affect Bargaining

1. Market reputation of builder/ developer- A well established builder sells his project in the launching stage so there is no scope for bargaining.
2. Condition of market/economy— you have more scope of bargaining, in case of any recession.
3. Whether developer has used his own funds or borrowed money from bank to develop the project. If he has used his own funds then he can hold on to the property and may not be ready for bargaining. If he has borrowed money from bank then he will be in hurry to sell the project and hence will be open to bargaining, because interest will continue increase the cost of construction. Sometimes, it is also important to investigate whether the land used for the project is self/leased or purchased.

The Lacuna when you are Purchasing a House

It is generally seen that people don't do proper homework before purchasing. Moreover they do not spend enough time in understanding the developer and his past project. Due to this lack of research, they are unable to bargain well.

Art of Bargaining

Listen carefully and do proper due diligence regarding facts. Keep silent during bargaining and note all the things and offer a realistic rate. You should keep a sanction letter with cheque book ready so that the developers don't underestimate you and consider you as a prospective buyer.

Opportunity

1. First of all, get a provisional sanction letter from bank because this will convince the developers that you mean business.
2. Prepare a group of property buyers. The members of this group may be your friends or colleagues or your relatives. Group bookings are preferred by developers because it helps them to sell more flats in a single deal and the members of the group get good discount.
3. Decide your budget.
4. Survey the location where you are going to purchase the property. Talk to the people who are presently living there and try to find out the present market rate of the property. If you find that a lot of flats are vacant due to a slump in the market, try bargaining with the builder..
5. The best places for getting great discounts are property carnivals and property fairs. These are the places where you can look at all the properties around your city.

Bargaining Procedure

Let us assume that you have decided to purchase a particular flat in a particular apartment. Now, you are sitting with the builder in his office. You have a cheque book in your hand and you are asking him to quote his 'best price' (maximum possible lowest price of the flat to be purchased). At this stage, when the builder quotes the minimum price then you should quote a lower but realistic price.

When bargaining, offer a price which is realistic. Do not offer a price which is impossible for the builder. Once you have quoted your lower but realistic offer and if he does not agree, you can ask him to think about the offer or tell him that you will rethink about deal later.

Always keep a flexible approach because your main aim is to purchase the property not to defeat builder in bargaining. If you like the offer, then accept it. Moreover, if you and your family members really like the flat and can afford the price, then don't bargain so much that you lose the deal completely. Step back and analyze the situation and work accordingly.

❑

26

Agreement to Sale

An Agreement to sale is a contract between two parties in which one party agrees to sell something to the other party on a future date. Sale is defined as the transfer of ownership in exchange for a price paid and part promised. Normally the sale agreement is done either when you purchase a new flat/villa/commercial space from a builder or a resale property from any individual. As per the Indian law, the transfer by way of sale of tangible immovable property of the value of rupee one hundred and above can be made by a registered instrument.

Development authorities and Housing Boards issue allotment letters instead of agreement to sale.

Read the Sale Agreement Carefully Before Signing It

Searching for a property is a time consuming process. It can take months, even years, to find your dream house. After extensive bargaining, when you manage to close the deal, you have to do an agreement to sale with builder or seller. When agreement to sale is ready (in case you purchase a flat/villa from builder then the agreement is normally drafted by builder), remember to read the agreement carefully before signing on it.

Once the agreement to sale is signed and stamped, a sale deed is drafted on the basis of agreement to sale. The contract is binding on both the parties, and if any one of them fails to fulfill their commitment, it automatically gives the other party the right to term the contract null and void. Read the documents and avoid making any payments or signing the documents if you are unsure. In their hurry to get the paperwork done, buyers often miss the important clauses that sellers and builders slip into a sale agreement. Remember sale agreements are full of important clauses and you should read and understand each of these very carefully before signing them otherwise you may land up in a soup.

Make sure you check important facts like your name, age, father's name, residential address and the PAN number printed on the agreement. You should also check and confirm the flat number with floor number and block number in the township listed in the agreement.

For example in an agreement that says flat no-A-1010 on tenth floor, 'A' represent the block number of the township.

Please check the undermentioned topics before signing the agreement to sale.

1. **Right to alter specifications:** When you visit the site where project is being constructed the sales person of company shows you a sample flat. Basically sample flat is marketing tool to attract customers so that company can increase its sale. They are demolished immediately after the flats are sold out or building is ready for possession. Some builders often slip in a clause stating that they can alter the layout plan of the flat or apartment that was shown to you. Hence, the final flat layout may be quite different from the sample flat that you saw at the time of booking. The sample flat can appear to be much larger than the real one. You will not be able to drag the builder to consumer court if the agreement

contains a clause stating that the builder can change the specifications.

A Smart Option

Always consider the actual drawing, because sample flats are only indicative. Generally these are furnished with furniture and fixtures and sometimes they may be slightly larger compare to an actual flat. Once the architectural plans are approved by the development authority or local Municipal Corporation, the builder cannot change them without their consent. If a builder promises to use a certain brand of fixtures in the flat, you should insist that he clearly mentions this in the agreement.

2. **Area of the flat/house:** There are three basic ways in which the area of a house can be measured: super area, built-up area and carpet area. The super area includes the proportionate share of common facilities, such as the lobby, corridors and staircases. The built-up area is the size of the apartment, including the walls. The carpet area is the actual size of the apartment. Builders should ideally mention the carpet area in the agreement, but they almost always state the super built-up area that is 20-30% more than the carpet area.

What can you do?

Insist on finding out the carpet area of the house. Take a look at the building plans, so that you know the real size of the living space that you will get in the apartment. Check whether the carpet area mentioned in agreement is in accordance to the deal and builder's promises or not.

3. **Additional charges:** An advertisement in a newspaper states '2BHK flat is available for ₹25 lakh only'. Friends, when you approach the builder to book the flat, you will find that it costs around ₹30 lakh. The property prices stated in advertisements are only the base prices. The actual amount that the buyer may have to shell out is 20-35% higher. Park

facing and garden facing flats are more expensive than the regular flats. Gym membership, car parking, common utilities and maintenance charges add up to a significant sum.

Option for you

One of my seniors Mr. Yogendra Souhaya booked a ground floor flat in a township. During booking of the flat he was told that he would be provided 16 square meters extra land. It was mentioned in booking confirmation letter. But when he was signing the agreement to sale, he observed that 16 meters extra land was not mentioned in agreement to sale. He insisted that the company should mention the same on the letter. The company officers told him that they can state this on a letter bearing the company's letter head but cannot mention it in agreement to sale because as per their specifications, the purchaser could only use the land. Always remember that developers don't offer any facility free of cost. Make a list of the charges you will have to pay and get the builder to sign it. Most of the developers would be cautious about giving anything in writing if they have something to hide.

4. **Payment plan clause:** Payment plan is finalized at the time of booking. You must check whether the payment plan decided by you is mentioned in agreement to sale and all dates of future payments or installments to builder are as per the plan. You should examine closely before signing it.

   Check the date of payment to builder with grace period, amount to be paid and the penalty clause. Normally builders include a penalty clause if you fail to deposit the installment on time. They generally charge at the rate of 18% p.a. If some advance has been paid to the builder, the amount and mode of payment should be mentioned in the agreement.

   What can you do?

   If you have applied for a home loan from bank then keep in mind that the bank will disburse a proportionate amount of loan. Suppose, the cost of flat is ₹25 lakh and loan amount is ₹20 lakh. If builder installment is ₹1 lakh then you have to introduce your margin of ₹20,000 in it. So before purchasing, make a realistic estimate of your payment capacity of loan as well as margin arrangement and buy only if you are sure that you can afford it. Before paying the installment to builder, visit the project site and check whether the demand is in accordance to the construction stage of the building.

5. **Tax payment:** Friends, keep in mind that the registration charges and service tax are to be paid by you. However, it is the builder's responsibility to pay property tax before handing over the possession to you.

   Option for you

   Sort out this issue before the agreement is signed. Clarify with the builder about who will pay the taxes and have it incorporated in the agreement.

6. **Is there an escalation clause?**

   You should avoid projects which have an escalation clause. Builders often include a cost-escalation clause in the builder-buyer agreement. It says that if the cost of building materials or other inputs goes up, the developer reserves the right to hike the cost of the project. State Housing Boards normally mention this clause in application form. Since they are controlled by state government so need not be worry. Make enquiries regarding the builder's track record; has he implemented escalation clause in the past? Did he have a genuine reason to implement the clause? Or, opt for a developer who does not include an escalation clause in the agreement to sale.

7. **When will the project be completed? Or what is the delivery date?**

   Normally developers construct project-phase wise so that they can fulfill their commitment on time.The agreement to sale usually states that the project will be completed within a certain period. Usually, this period varies 36-42 months from the construction start date. However, if no explicit starting date is mentioned in the agreement, you should send an e-mail to the developer and get a written reply from him regarding the starting date of the project. Developers tend to give a rough time frame within which they will hand over the possession of the property to the buyer.

You should try to ensure that builder mentions a clear cut month and year of possession. It is in the interest of the potential buyer that the purchase agreement includes a clause which mentions the date on or before which the developer will hand over the possession of his property.

8. **Is there a penalty clause regarding delay in possession of flat?**

   Just as the builder may levy a penalty for delay in payment on your part, you can incorporate the penalty that the builder must pay if he delays handing over the possession on schedule. In case of a delay in handing over possession, the developer pays a penalty to the buyer, provided the penalty clause has been incorporated in the builder-buyer agreement. Find out how much penalty he will pay. Also, when there was a delay in the past, did he pay the penalty or did he find a way to circumvent it? If the project is delayed, then make a group of customers who are facing a similar problem and talk to the builder. If he still does not listen, you can go to the media and consumer court.

9. **Assignment or transfer:** If you are purchasing a flat for residential purpose, then this clause is not a problem for you. But if you are doing an investment, then consider this clause. Builders usually mention this clause to restrict your ability to transfer or assign your property to a third person without their prior permission till the housing society is

formed. Therefore, it may be difficult for you to sell your property before the housing society is formed. Even after the society is formed, you may require a no-objection certificate from the society to sell your property.

Option for you

Ideally, you should avoid transferring the property before the society is formed because it is easier to deal with a property where the society has been created and share certificates have been issued to members. However, legally speaking, a builder cannot ask you to pay a penalty for transferring the property to a third person.

Resale Property

1. **Earnest money/Token Money:** A token payment is generally made to a seller showing the buyer's good faith in a transaction. Often used in real estate transactions, earnest money allows the buyer additional specified time period to arrange the remaining amount of money. If he fails to make the balance payment within the time frame agreed upon, he foregoes the earnest money given to the seller.

   Sometimes, sellers insist that this should be mentioned in the sale agreement. In such a case, make sure everything is explicitly stated, along with the date by which the payment has to be made. The amount received as token money must also be clearly mentioned. Always try to pay it in the form of cheques or demand draft.

   Friends, if you are purchasing a property then you should also mention in the agreement that if the seller backs out of the deal, he will not only return the earnest money but also pay an equal amount as compensation to the buyer.

What can you do?

Assess your capacity to pay the balance amount within the deadline before you commit to it.Try not to pay more than 2% of the sale consideration of the property as token money. Even if you need to back out of the deal, you won't lose a large amount. It's a good idea to mention the circumstances under which you can exit without losing the token amount. For instance, you may find that the carpet area is smaller than claimed or there are problems with the structure.

2. **No access to property:** Generally, a buyer is allowed to inspect the property before the deal is closed. However, you may not be satisfied with a single visit and may want an expert to accompany you. Some of your relatives may also want to visit the property. This won't be possible if there is a no-access clause in the agreement. Till the final payment has not been made, you cannot force the seller to allow you into the house whenever you want. However, you should be entitled to inspect the property before registry.

   What can you do?

   If the property is vacant, the seller may not have a problem if the buyer wants to visit it again. However, if it is occupied by him or an existing tenant, then going there too often can be inconvenient. So make sure the agreement mentions a mutually suitable time for you to visit the property. It is mandatory to ensure that the property is vacant before registry as sometimes a cunning owner or tenant may refuse to vacate it once he gets the money.

3. **'As is, where is' basis:** Sometimes you read an advertisement related to bank auction regarding selling of property stating 'as is, where is' basis. Normally banks don't spend money on the repair of property. In such cases, the sale is on an 'as is, where is' basis, which means the property is being

offered in its existing condition. The buyer is free to inspect the property before participation in auction but once the deal is inked, the seller is not responsible for any damage that may be discovered after the purchase.

4. **If property is vacant or on Lease:** Commercial properties are leased out for some years. If you purchase such a property then you must mention the lease details in the agreement to sale so that the change in ownership does not create problems either for the buyer or the lessee. It is also important that you mention who will get the rent. Sometimes, there may be an arrangement that the seller would get the rent till the lease expires. Any such arrangement must be explicitly mentioned in the contract.

   What can you do?

   Friends, it is always advisable that you should get house or property vacated before sale deed execution. Make sure there is no ambiguity regarding the person who gets to keep the rent. If you plan to get a new tenant, send a notice to the existing one to vacate the property. Also, the agreement should clearly specify the date by which the lessee must vacate the property.

5. **Always mention if property is already mortgaged with the Bank:** Sometimes you may purchase a property which is already mortgaged with a bank or a non banking finance company. The seller may have availed a housing loan or loan against property. Purchasing this property may not be so easy because it involves a lender as a third party.

   Now there are two situations; the seller is capable of repaying the loan and may execute sale deed or he can also use the advance money paid by you to prepay the loan and the bank can release the property's original papers. Sometimes the seller has no fund and he may directly ask you to close the loan.

In this situation, you may take home loan from the same bank as the seller so that the bank directly adjusts the loan by disbursing your loan to seller's loan account. In many instances, even if you select another bank, then the new one can also disburse the loan to the loan account of the seller but it may ask for any security or third party guarantee up to a period till you get your property registered. After closing his loan, you may execute a sale deed with seller and deposit it in the bank. Whichever option you choose, do not forget to state it in the agreement. Mention the complete loan details. If you have paid the entire loan, you should mention it under the no-dues clause too.

6. **Check whether there are Any Dues and get No Dues:** Normally agreement to sale has a clause that property has no any dues and if any dues occur then this will be settled by seller. It means that the property has no pending dues against it, including society maintenance charges, utility bills, taxes or other loans. Always make sure that seller clears up all the dues before sale deed execution.

   Always check the latest water and electricity bills. Also check that if there is any pending payments as far as lease money or house tax on the property are concerned. Find out from the housing society, if there are any pending charges before you finalize the deal. The society may refuse to give a no-objection certificate for the sale if there are pending dues on the flat by the owner, which may obstruct the smooth transfer of the property.

❑

27

Registry and Possession

Most buyers book a residential property hoping that they will soon be living in their dream home.

Normally the registry is done as soon as buyer gets possession of flat. If any builder does not do the registry post the buyer's possession, it can be termed as an illegal act.

- **Possession:** Possession can be defined as when buyer gets the keys of the house from developer and moves into his house.
- **Registry /Sale deed:** It is a document which contains the legal agreement drawn between the buyer and the seller. It transfers legal rights of flat from builder/ seller to buyer. It should be registered in registrar office after paying stamp duty (usually between 5% and 12.5% across India.) to the government. The registration of a document serves as a notice of the transaction to the person affected by the transaction. Registration also serves as an implied notice to any person subsequently acquiring interest in the property, covered by the registered document.

If You Buy a Flat from a Builder

If you buy a flat from a builder, generally all formalities including the registry from the buyer's side are done by builders. At that time buyer should keep eye on all the activities by the builder. Otherwise buyer may be in trouble. When the draft of registry is ready then ask the builder to provide a copy of draft. Read this draft carefully. It is a good idea that you take the help of an advocate who is an expert in real estate matters to know whether all the things which are mentioned in agreement to sale are also present in the draft.

Normally, builders try to hand over possession of a flat to buyers as soon as possible but a project may get delayed for six months to one year. Many reputed developers mention the expected date of possession in agreement to sale. They also mention a clause for another six months as a grace period due to some unavoidable circumstances like labor strike, recession, some government issues, environmental issues (ban on raw material supply), etc.

Buyers who have booked their flats generally live in rented accommodations. They create a pressure on builder to get possession soon. Due to this pressure, builder gives the possession of the flats without registry. However, without the registry the buyer cannot be termed as the owner of the flat.

Why Developers delay in Registry?

When a project is ready along with all the functioning facilities (road, lift, garden, gym, swimming pool etc) then the local development authority issues a completion certificate. After receiving the completion certificate, builder can do the registry of flats. In this scenario, the pending work of the apartment continues and the buyer can also live in his house.

What are the problems if you take possession without registry?

After taking the possession, the speed of completion slows down and the builder may ask the buyer to pay additional charges for other facilities. In this situation, the buyer will be forced to pressure to accept the builder's demand as he may be scared that the builder may cause problems at the time of the registry.

When to do the registry and what precautions must be kept in mind?

Always take possession after registry. Before signing the sale deed of flat or apartment, it should be fully completed. If you have taken possession without registry then do the registry within six months of possession. Always check if all facilities like parking, common area, transformer, generator charges are included.

Documents Needed for Registration

- **From the developer:** In case of a newly built apartment complex, the builder needs to obtain a completion certificate from the local authority. This certificate will be given to you along with the possession letter.
- **From the seller:** Apart from the sale deed, you will need the property tax papers and a letter from the housing society, which states that the housing society has no objection and that you are the new owner of the property and have paid the society's transfer fee.
- **Your documents:** You will need a copy of the PAN card, Aadhar card, photo identity proof (passport/driving license), and proof of residence, along with signatures of two witnesses. If you have a home loan, you will need a no-objection certificate from lender.

Why you should get your house registered soon?

- **Requirement:** According to section 17 of the Indian Registration Act, 1908, it is mandatory to register the documents regarding the transfer, sale or lease of property.
- **Time limit:** According to section 23 of Act, you need to register the property within four months of executing the sale/gift deed.
- **Penalty:** In case of delay, Section 34 of the Act allows you to register the property in the next four months by paying the charges along with a penalty.

Procedure involved in mutation of property

There are various documents that the seller of a residential property has to hand over to the buyer at the time of sale of property. In this regard, the prospective buyer often requests the seller to provide the latest mutation of the residential property. Hence, it is imperative that the seller is aware of this document and its relevance in the context of the sale of his property.

What does mutation of property mean?

Mutation of property involves the change of title ownership of the property from the seller to the buyer when it is sold or transferred. The title of the property is then recorded in the land revenue records in the new owner's name, which then enables the government to collect property taxes from the rightful owner.

Procedure

Ideally, the updates regarding mutation of property should be taken every six months through the land revenue office to check whether any wrongful transaction that has been undertaken on the property in question. The documentation procedure and the fee that has to be paid to the revenue office for mutation of property varies from one state to another. In general, the procedure involves an application that has to be submitted to the officer of that particular area on a plain paper. Along with the application, a non-judicial stamp of relevant value (as per the state norms where the land is located) should be included along with the required information.

❑

28

Real Estate Regulation Act (RERA)

Real estate regulation act was first notified in March 2016 for bringing-in greater transparency and protection of consumer rights in the real estate sector. Under this act, no promoter shall advertise, market, book, sell or offer for sale, or invite persons to purchase in any manner any plot, apartment or building, without registering the project with the Real Estate Regulatory Authority.

This act also made provisions for on-going projects which have not received completion certificate, to apply for registration within three months of commencement of the act.

Provisions of the act include:

- For speedy and formulated implementation of this law, each state is mandated to form a Real Estate Appellate tribunal within the period of 1 year from the commencement of the act.
- Depositing 70 per cent of the funds collected from buyers in a separate bank account in case of new projects and 70 per cent of unused funds in case of ongoing projects.

- Any project with a plot size of 500 sq. Mt or 8 apartments shall mandatorily register itself with RERA.
- Builder cannot take advance as a booking amount of more than 10 % of sale consideration from any buyer. If he takes, then he has to do a written agreement.
- Both developer and the buyer will be liable to pay penal interest of SBI's marginal cost of lending rate+ 2 % in case of delay in payments.
- Imprisonment of up to three years for developers and up to one year in case of agents and buyers for violation of orders of Appellate Tribunals and Regulatory Authorities.
- Pre-launch –booking is prohibited.
- Builder can sell flats on carpet area basis.

Benefits of this law to consumer, developer and real estate agent:

- **Gains to buyers:** Buyers will benefit from greater transparency and defined laws under this act which would protect buyer's interest and enhance customer confidence in the real estate sector. As per the law, 70 per cent of the funds taken by the buyer should be kept in the separate bank account which is security call for individual's money. This would also mitigate the risks of diversion of the buyer's money towards projects other than for their respective investment. Also, buyer's consent for making any structural reform in the project has strengthened the rights of consumers. These regulations will bring-in buyer confidence and contribute in stabilizing housing prices.
- **Gains to builders:** Builders will also enjoy a regulated framework for dealing with the projects. These regulations would remove the unhealthy competition and protect the rights of a genuine builder. Builder can also lodge their complaint against the buyer who is not paying the dues on time and impose penal Interest on the same. These

structural reforms would channelize the investment and thereby generating healthy demand and better prospects for emerging builders.

- **Gains to banking sector:** Banking sector would also benefit from pick-up in demand for housing and regulated framework. This law would help in business generation and maintaining proper due diligence for the builders which would aid in mitigating the generation of fresh bad assets in this sector. Under this regulation, increase in housing demand would help in credit pick-up to this sector. Also, builders would park 70 per cent of the fund with banks which would generate current account for banks.
- **Gains to economy:** Economy as a whole would benefit from this law along with benefits to each participants of the sector. First, regulated environment would mitigate the illegal flow of money and thereby regulating the prices. Second, tax collection from this sector is expected to nearly double coming from proper channels and registered builders. Also, on an average, about 10 lakh buyers invest every year for owing a house. Stringent laws and defined regulatory structure would enhance the growth of this sector and contribute to overall GDP in the future.

Conclusion

Implementation of this law has been a historic move in real estate sector of the economy. Sighting the overall gains to economy, this law has been a welcome move to revive the sector. Its final implementation from May 01, 2017 was a unanimous decision of both the centre and state. Henceforth, any project imitated would go to respective states' real estate tribunal and case-by-case review would be put-in place. These developments together benefit the economy for greater transparency and stringent regulatory framework.

❑

29

Circle Rate & Black Money in Real Estate

When you are going to purchase a property (plot/ house/ flat/ shop), you must always consider the Market Rate and Circle Rate/DLC Rate (District Level Committee Rate). Now it is necessary for you to understand these rates.

Market Rate

This is the rate which is settled between the buyer and the seller of the property. This rate is dependent on demand and supply of the property in the market. The more the demand, higher the price and lesser the demand lower the price. Where demand is more than the supply, market rate is high. It is also dependent on the basic infrastructure of that particular area, development of markets, recreation facilities, school, hospital, security and other facilities in that area.

Circle Rate/ DLC Rate

Circle rate is the minimum rate defined by all the state governments at which a property can be bought or sold. Circle rates put a check on the speculation of property prices. Within a state, there are different circle rates for different cities and within a city, circle rates vary according to the locality. This rate is normally decided by Revenue Department of State Government or Local Development Authority. Agricultural land, commercial property and residential property have different circle rates. Circle Rate increases from time to time. Normally it is used as reference rate. Its basic purpose is to determine the stamp duty at the time of registry.

Normally in the Indian property market, market rates are higher than circle rates due to the following reasons:

1. Circle rate is not reviewed regularly while market rate is dependent on demand and supply.
2. Circle rate is under the control of local development authority or State Governments.
3. Circle rate does not show the real price of property as it is applicable for stamp duty consideration which means you have to pay stamp duty as per the circle rate.

While calculating the stamp duty with respect to the sale transactions which are to be registered in the office of Sub Registrar, the value on which such stamp duty is to be calculated is not necessarily the figure mentioned in the sale deed; it could be a much higher figure than the sale price agreed to between the buyer and the seller. This might sound somewhat absurd, but it is true.

This is because the stamp duty is calculated on the actual purchase consideration, or the circle rate, whichever is higher. Whenever you buy any property, you must enquire in advance from the office of the Sub Registrar about the current Circle Rate/DLC Rate of the property.

Sub Registrar offices are located in different parts of India and each of these maintain a chart of circle rate prevalent in the area. This chart of circle rate clearly mentions the minimum rate which will be considered by the Sub Registrar for the purposes of charging stamp duty with respect to the property.

Thus, even if purchase price of the property is lower than the circle rate, stamp duty would be payable as per the valuation based on the circle rate. The Circle Rate chart as mentioned by the Sub Registrar's office contains details about fair valuation of the property in rural areas as well as in urban areas. This Circle Rate chart also contains the system of valuation not merely of the vacant land but even of the constructed portion of the building or flat.

Thus, the stamp duty is payable on the circle rate of the property in a particular area. If the property which you are buying is only partially built-up, the Sub Registrar will value the property based on the facts and circumstances. He may even ask the buyer/seller to submit a valuation report from the architect so that fair assessment can be done with respect to transferred property..

There are certain provisions under Section 50C of the Income-tax Act, 1961 with respect to the seller of the property, the sale price of the property is not what is mentioned in the sale deed but the price as per the relevant circle rate by the stamp valuation authority for the purpose of payment of stamp duty in respect of transfer of the property. This is the case when the circle rate is higher than price in consideration. In such a case, the seller of the property is also required to pay tax with respect to the capital gains on a higher amount because the Circle Rate is actually substituted for the actual sale consideration.

Let us take an example. Mr. Ravi was owner of a residential house. He sold his property to Mr. Mohan for ₹100 lakh but drew up a sale agreement for ₹50 lakh. An additional amount of ₹50 lakh was received in cash, which was not declared.

During the process of registration, the officer in the office of sub registrar found that agreement was less than circle rate (Rs 60 lakh), so he charged stamp duty on ₹60 lakh instead of ₹50 lakh. Further, at the time of calculation of capital gain, Mr. Ravi had to consider ₹60 lakh as sale consideration instead of ₹50 lakh as per provisions of Section 50C. This fact created higher income tax liability on account of capital gains.

To avoid such a situation, some cunning property buyers purchase a property on the basis of Power of Attorney and Agreement to Sell. However, most banks and NBFCs in the country don't give loan advances for buying a property through Power of Attorney.

Thus, it is always better to buy the property by getting the same registered with the Sub Registrar office and also by making payments of the stamp duty charges based on the prevailing circle rate or the actual purchase price, whichever is higher. As per the Finance (No. 2) Act, 2009 the provisions of Section 50C would be applicable even with respect to Power of Attorney and Agreement to Sell Transactions.

Reserve Price

When a local development authority decides to sell a government's plots in an auction, it decides a minimum rate of property on which auction starts. This is known as the reserve price.

Black Money in Real Estate

Who is Responsible? Lower Circle Rate?

In property purchasing cases, stamp duty is normally paid by the buyer. When the difference between the property's market rate and circle rate is less, the property does not attract many investors. Thus only real buyers are interested in purchasing the property for residential purposes.

Lower circle rate helps the corrupt to convert black money into white money. If government increases circle rate up to market rate, then the government may earn more revenue from stamp duty as well as from capital gain.

The actual property rates per unit area in the real world are usually higher than the benchmark circle rates, and that is how black money changes hands among the property sellers and buyers. The property sellers and buyers tend to show lower valuations of the properties thereby trying to save a quantum of registration fee and stamp duty that one needs to pay to the government.

❑

30

Rent Agreement

A rent agreement/leave agreement and license agreement are often used interchangeably, but in fact there is a significant difference between the two.

Lease agreement/Rental Agreement/Tenancy Agreement

This agreement comes under State Rent Control Act Section 105 of 'The Transfer of Property Act, 1882,' Lease is defined as a transfer of the rights to enjoy the concerned property for a pre-defined time period or in perpetuity. The Lesser (owner of the property) gives the Lessee (the one leasing the property) such consideration periodically, usually at the beginning or end of a lease agreement.

Leave & License Agreement

License is defined in Section 52 of the Indian Easements Act 1882. License does not allow any interest in the premises on the licensee's part. It merely gives the licensee the right to use and occupy the premises for a limited duration. It comes under local rent control act. Normally landlords prefer this type of agreement. It has minimum period of 11 months. It may be renewed further. If tenure is more than 11 months, it must be registered in office of sub-registrar.

A lease deed needs to be stamped and registered. The amount payable towards the lease deed's stamp duty is more than that payable towards the Leave and License's. For a period exceeding three years, the stamp duty is same for both agreements.

A person, who does not own a house in a particular city and wants to live in a rented house, is called a tenant. If he has a house and wants to let it out, he is called a landlord.

If you are a Tenant

You may require a house/flat on rent due to following reasons.

- You have been transferred in a city and you have to stay there for 3 to 5 years. It means you don't see yourself living in the same place for a long time.
- You may be required to move at a short notice.
- You are not sure of which house to buy.
- You don't have funds for down payment.
- You can't afford the purchase or you cannot afford the upkeep of the house.

When Vahid Khan a 31- year old banker finalized a house on rent at Gopalpura Bypass in Jaipur two years ago, he thought he would stay there for 2-3 years till he bought his own flat or got transferred to another city. The house was in a reasonably good condition and was very close to his bank. So, he immediately signed the agreement with the landlord. Vahid had agreed to pay a monthly rent of ₹6,000 and handed over ₹18,000 (three months advance) as deposit money.

However, six months later, the landlord wanted to increase the rent by ₹1000 as there was sudden increase of students in that area as the rent in the area shot up due to an increase in the number of coaching classes in that area. He had two options, pay the extra money or hunt for another house. His landlord told him that such an increase was a norm. Moreover, no clause to this effect was mentioned in the lease agreement. Since it was difficult to look for another house in such a short notice, he paid the extra amount.

Before you Sign a Rent Agreement

Vahid could have avoided this hassle if he had scrutinized the rent agreement carefully before signing it and made changes that could have served his interests better. However, most tenants are not even aware of the points that should be included in the rent agreement.

Let us discuss each point in detail.

Is the lesser the actual owner of property?

Mr. Raghu is a senior executive in a multinational company which is located in Bangalore. He is facing a case of trespassing (entering in a building that you don't have permission or the right to enter) in a local court. Last year he was transferred to Bangalore and he finalized a big house for rent. Basically this house belongs to a NRI who lives in London. His caretaker in India Mr. D'Souza who was a cunning person drafted a rent agreement showing him as an owner. Mr. Raghu signed the agreement without scrutinizing the title papers of property.

Mr. D'Souza had slyly inserted a clause stating, "The tenant has verified the title papers of the house and confirmed and satisfied that Mr. D'Souza is the rightful owner of the house". Friends, if you fail to check the agreement carefully and sign it, you could be held liable for trespassing. When NRI came to India he asked Mr. Raghu to evict the house immediately. However, Raghu refused to vacate since it was exam time for his children. The NRI filed a case of trespassing against Raghu. Mr. Raghu couldn't challenge eviction in this case.

Always read rent agreement carefully. If this clause was not mentioned in rent agreement then Mr. Raghu could hold Mr. D'Souza responsible for cheating and committing fraud. Before you sign the agreement, make sure that the person you are transacting with is the actual owner of the property. Otherwise it would create a problem for you. Sometimes, investors or NRIs appoint caretakers for their property, who may lease it to a third party without the knowledge of the owner.

So, you should verify the property papers such as the, lease deed or sale deed. If this house or flat is situated in a housing society then ask the landlord to show you the share certificate. You should obtain no-objection- certificate (NOC) from the housing society where you want to live on rent. These papers will assure you that you are dealing with the right person. Utility bills are also helpful because they show the owner's name on it. While you are at it, make sure to peruse the papers that state the property tax has been paid by the landlord.

Sometimes the landlord may have taken a loan from the bank and the apartment is mortgaged. Hence, the original sale deed will be in the custody of the bank. In such a case, an NOC should be obtained from the bank. This will mention the rightful owner's name.

Duration of Agreement & Renewal Condition

A rent agreement includes the terms and conditions under which the house/flat is given on rent. It specifies the rent per month and the tenure for which the agreement is made, as well as the security amount that needs to be deposited with the landlord by the tenant. The agreement should also clearly mention the day before which the rent is expected to be paid. For instance, it could be the 5th or 10th of every month. If the tenant fails to pay the rent before the predetermined period, the penal charges that he would be liable to pay should also be defined in the agreement.

The tenure of a rent agreement is usually for 11 months, unless otherwise specified in the contract. If it is for more than a year, it's mandatory for landlord to get the agreement registered. The agreement should contain the notice period and penalty for cancelling the agreement without completing the specified period. Typically, a two-month notice is served in case of high rental properties, while one month's notice is sufficient for low rental ones.

Condition of Increment of Rent

Earlier we have discussed the problem faced by Mr. Vahid. A tenant should verify whether the owner has included a rent escalation clause in the agreement, which could be used to increase the rent after a certain months. The best way to safeguard yourself is to ensure that the agreement specifies the dates on which the rent escalation will be applicable and the percentage of increase. For example, rent will be increased @ rate of 5% per renewal/year. This will save you from hassles which Vahid faced.

Water, Electricity & Other monthly Expenditure Payment condition

The rent agreement could also mention the facilities, such as parking space or the usage of society's gym, included with the property. There could also be additional monthly charges, such as the society maintenance charge and club fee. It's best if the additional charges for using such facilities are clearly spelt out, along with the person who is supposed to bear them. If either party fails to honor the terms and conditions of the agreement, it will become void, and the aggrieved party could claim penal charges.

Notice Period and Cancellation Clause

You should also make sure that there is a clause on the sale of the house. If the owner decides to sell the house during the term of the rent agreement, the notice period should be clearly defined in the agreement. This is important because as a tenant you need time to search for another accommodation.

Before you sign the agreement, it is also important to check if all the switches and the connections in the house are working properly. If you discover a problem after signing the agreement or fail to check a minor repair work for installed electrical appliances, then it is your responsibility to get the fault repaired and pay for it. However, if the property is damaged because of negligence on your part, the landlord can rightfully use the security money deposited with him for carrying out the necessary renovation.

You also have the right to see the documents that prove all previous bills related to the house have been paid, especially the electricity, water and gas bills.

If you are a Landlord

Conduct background checks

It is important to check the antecedents of a potential tenant before signing the agreement. You can ask for a reference certificate from the tenant, and also enquire from his previous landlord or employer. Make sure you ask for valid permanent address or gas connection document since it may be useful if you need to track down the tenant. Lastly, check his office/business address and carefully go through the documents submitted.

Police Verification

Ignoring police verification is punishable offence under Section 188 of the Indian Penal Code. A background check is not enough; you need the official nod from the police. Indeed, tenant verification at a local police station is mandatory for all landlords. The landlord simply needs to fill in the details of the tenant like name, father name, age, permanent address, purpose of living on rent in the police verification form (available online in several states). This has to be submitted, along with the tenant's photo and copies of documents, such as PAN card, lease agreement and address proof, at the local police station. This reduces the risk of having tenants with a criminal background. A copy of this certificate needs to be submitted to your housing society office too.

Registering the lease agreement

If you are renting out your property for a few months then a lease agreement is not mandatory, but in case the renting out period is 11 months or more, then you need a lease agreement. This document contains details like tenure of the agreement, rent payable, deposit amount, any clauses that may result in cancellation of the agreement, and applicable penalty in case the tenant refuses to vacate. If you are planning to rent the property for more than a year, it is mandatory to get the lease agreement registered. This is a mandatory security measure for the landlord in case the tenant refuses to vacate or pay rent.

If your tenant refuses to vacate

You can face this problem if you have not done proper due diligence of tenant before letting out your house. When it comes to the relationship between landlord and a tenant, it's best to be safe than sorry. Prevention is better than cure. Yet, blindly trusting the brokers and being blinded by excessive rent offers are the main reasons for legal battles between landowners and rogue tenants. Take the case of Bangalore based Vikas Solanki. In 2006, he relied on a broker to lease his second home at Banergatta Road. The tenant family seemed decent and he thought it was completely safe to rent the property. However, his worst fears came true when the tenant refused to vacate the property after completing the year-long tenure.

He could not approach the police since it was a civil matter. So, Vikas approached the courts, and was told that the property would be vacated only if the judgment was in his favor.

As you know courts sometimes take a long time in deciding the case. However, Vikas was lucky because he was saved from waging a long legal battle when one of his acquaintances acted as an intermediate between the two parties and helped him settle the matter.

Exercising caution at the time of renting one's property is the only way to avoid being in the situation that Vikas and many others like him, find them in.

Grounds for eviction

A landlord can ask the tenant to leave if he has completed the tenure as per the lease agreement. Other valid grounds are refusal to pay the rent or indulging in unlawful activities on your property. You can demand eviction if the tenant has sub-let a part or all of your property without your permission. Unfortunately, due diligence in selection of a tenant and an iron-clad lease agreement are not a guarantee against legal hassles with rogue tenants. Sometimes your relatives and friends may suggest illegal means to avoid such hassles. For example opting for strong arm tactics or forcing the tenant to vacate the property using underhand techniques is illegal. It is also not advisable to shut off utilities like electricity or water connection in order to compel the tenant to vacate the property.

So what are your steps to resolve this situation?

- **Police can play a limited role:** Friends always remember that role of the police is limited. Police may help you if the tenant is involved in an illegal activity. However, it has no jurisdiction if the tenant refuses to vacate the premises or pay rent. The role of the police is to serve the court order of eviction to the tenant to vacate the house and if tenant after receiving court order refuses to vacate, then the police can use force to vacate the house.

- **Approach the designated authority in your state:** Under the Rent Control Act, every state government has appointed a competent authority to oversee disputes related to rented property within its borders. So a landlord is free to approach this body. He should carry with him all the registered documents since these can strengthen the case. The authority listens to both the parties and arrives at a decision. This process could take 5-6 months.
- **Approach the civil court if you are not satisfied with decision:** In case, either party is not satisfied with the decision given by the state competent authority, he may approach the small court or city civil court. There is no fixed period to sort things at this level. The case may go on for a year or two before the final decision is taken. If the judgment fails to satisfy you, then you can approach the high court.

❑

31

Co-Ownership in Rented Property

In India, many people purchase property in joint name. I have already explained that from the tax point of view when two or more than two person purchase a property in joint name they can take benefit from sections 80 c and 24 of the Income Tax Act. Now let us discuss another benefit of purchasing property in joint name. If you do so, then you can take advantage of the provisions of Section 26 of the Income Tax Act, 1961.

Let us look at the Section 26 of the Income Tax Act, 1961. This section is related to property which is jointly owned by two or more than two persons and having a rental income. The law states that where a property consisting of buildings or buildings and lands appurtenant thereto is owned by two or more persons and their respective shares are definite and ascertainable, such persons shall not in respect of such property be assessed as an association of persons, but the share of each such person in the income from the property as computed in accordance with sections 22 to 25 shall be included in his total income.

It is possible for a family to save income tax in respect of rental income received by letting out residential, commercial or industrial properties. When you purchase a property in joint name, you must clearly mention the percentage of ownership/ share of each co-owner in the sale deed and also confirm that each co-purchaser makes investment in the property equal to his/ or her share in the property. It means that each co-owner must contribute his or her separate funds for purchasing the property. If co-owners do not have sufficient funds for purchasing the property then they can take joint home loan from banks, NBFCs, friends and relatives. If you take loan from your spouse, always consider a reasonable rate of interest which is usually comparable to the rate of interest of a bank home loan.

Let us take an example of Mr. and Mrs. Saxena who are going to purchase a house of ₹50,00,000 in joint name and decided to take a joint home loan of ₹40,00,000 from bank. Now each of them should contribute ₹5,00,000 (total share by borrower is ₹10,00,000) from his or her savings account so that their equal share can be mentioned clearly in the registry. There is no restriction regarding the number of joint co-owners of the property.

When two or more than two persons jointly own a house/ flat/showroom/office space and let it out, then the rental income to be received will not be assessed as an association of persons but it is separately assessed in the income tax return of different co-owners in their respective hands.

Suppose you purchase a house in your name only and give it on rent for ₹50,000 per month so the rental income of the property is ₹6,00,000 p.a. You have also income from business or service. Imagine that your total income after clubbing of rental income crosses 20 % slab and your income tax payable would be at the highest slab of 30%. On the other hand, if the same property is jointly purchased by you and your family members (spouse, father, mother, brother), then their respective income from house property would be ₹3,00,000 for each. Now you are eligible for a lower income tax slab and each co-owner would be required to pay less income tax as compared to the earlier situation. In this way you may cut down the rate of income tax with respect to your income from house property.

But to take advantage of section 26 of income tax act 1961 you should keep in mind to always receive the rental income in separate names of all co- owners of property. It means that the rental income should not be received in the name of one person/ co-owner only. So always take the benefit of income tax laws, which help you to reduce your tax liability from rental income.

❑

32

Transfer of Property by Way of Gift Deed & Relinquishment Deed

One day Mrs. Vimla Devi Sharma w/o Late Shri Prakash Sharma, aged 45 years approached me for a housing loan. She had a photocopy of lease deed mentioned with three names, first her own name Mrs. Vimla Devi, second name Mr. Yash (son) aged 19 years third one Ms. Shreya (daughter) aged 23 years. She told me that earlier the property was in name of her husband and after his death the local development authority issued a lease deed in name of all three legal heirs. Now her daughter was married. She further told me that her daughter did not want any share in that property. She wanted to know what to do.

She also asked me for advice on how to transfer her daughter's share to her own name. Friends, now in this type of cases a sales deed may not always be a good idea, especially if you want to pass it on to relatives. In such cases, instruments like a gift deed or relinquishment deed can come to your rescue. However, blindly choosing either can lead to problems. You must understand the purpose of each deed before getting it drafted. Know the benefits as well as limitations of each. These documents are designed to play a specific role in the transfer of property and, hence, it is advisable to consult a financial planner or lawyer.

Sale Deed

It is the most common document used to transfer of immovable property. This is used between two parties, one seller and other purchaser/buyer. When a sale deed is executed one way transfer of money occurs. Its registration in office of sub registrar is compulsory where buyer has to pay stamp duty as per state stamp act.

Gift Deed

This document allows you to gift your assets or transfer ownership without any exchange of money. To gift immovable property, you just have to draft the document on a stamp paper and should be attested by two witnesses. Registration of gift deed in the office of sub registrar is mandatory as per Section 17 of the registration Act, 1908, failing which the transfer will be invalid. This type of transfer is irrevocable. It means if you have gifted your property to your relative, it will be the property of the beneficiary and you cannot reverse the transfer or even ask for monetary compensation.

However, if you want to gift movable property like jewelry, paintings, registration is not compulsory. But entry in an account book as well as physical handing over the property is compulsory. Support this action with drafting a gift deed. If you gift property to certain relatives (your spouse, you or your spouse's lineal ascendant or descendent, brothers and sisters of either of your parents, in case of HUF any member belonging to the family and your spouse's sibling) they will not be taxed. But gift deeds to non-relatives are taxable.

Advantages

The biggest benefit is that there is no tax implication if you are gifting property to certain relatives. Stamp duty is applicable when a property is gifted. Stamp duty can vary from 1-8% for immovable property, depending on the state in which the transfer takes place. If you are gifting property to a non-relative, the stamp duty would be higher at 5-11%.

Drawbacks

Though a gift deed cannot be revoked, it can be challenged in court, coercion and fraud being the most common grounds. So, if you have been tricked into gifting property, you can take the matter to court and have the transfer reversed. It can also be challenged on the grounds that the donor was not of sound mind or a minor. You can never have a challenge-free gift deed, but consult a lawyer while drafting it so that the chances of it being challenged are minimum. Also, you cannot gift a property that is held jointly. If you and your spouse have a property in joint name then you can't gift it without the legal consent of your spouse.

Relinquishment Deed

Drafting this type of deed is the only answer for Mrs. Vimla Devi's question. This document is quite different from a gift deed, though the legal implications are the same. Relinquishment deed is a legal document in which a legal heir gives up or releases his legal rights in an inherited or parental property in favor of other legal heirs such as brother, mother, father or sister etc. The term 'Relinquishment' refers to the abandoning and surrender of the rights, title and interest, by one co-owner of a property in favor of the other co-owners. It means share of one co-owner increases.

You can use this instrument if you want to transfer your rights in a particular property to another co-owner. Such a transfer is also irrevocable even if it is without any exchange of money. As with all documents related to the transfer of immovable property, a relinquishment deed needs to be signed by both parties. Remember that the registration of relinquishment deed is compulsory as per section 17 of the Registration act 1908. The stamp duty is similar to that for gift deed. However, there is no discount for relatives, nor are there any tax benefits. Also, both stamp duty and tax will be applicable only on the portion of the property that you relinquish, not on its total value.

Advantages

It allows seamless transfer of your share in a jointly owned property. This document is most commonly used when a person dies without leaving behind a will and all siblings end up inheriting the property. In such a case, relinquishment deed is used for transferring the shares of the legal heirs in favor of one of them and then getting the Mutation done in favor of the legal heir in the records of local development authority. Unlike a gift deed, you can draw the relinquishment deed for monetary consideration. In India after death of both parents, their daughters normally relinquish their share with help of this deed in favor of their brothers.

Drawbacks

There are no tax benefits, for as per the tax laws, the term 'transfer' includes relinquishment, not gift. Hence, when you are relinquishing property for monetary consideration, it will result in capital gains for the transferor.

❑

33

What should you do before Selling a Property?

If you have made any investment in real estate, than you must know that, an investment in real estate is only advantageous when you do it for at least 3 to 5 years. Real estate cannot make a person rich overnight. After investing and understanding the cycles and the up downs of the real estate, you need to decide if you want to stay in it or exit.

Don't consider flip (flip means to purchase a property and resell it when the price appreciates).

You have to understand the macro and micro market cycle. You should be very familiar with advantages and drawbacks of real estate. You should also know the right time to exit it so that you can earn profit from it. Every industry has a cycle. During this cycle a business may be on the top or bottom. Just like that real estate has also a cycle which can be used to earn profit. Purchase the property when prices are low and sell the property when prices are high. In the real estate cycle, there is a time when property prices are increasing rapidly. At that time keep an eye on your investments. The investments in that particular time may be risky. Falling prices offer a chance to invest.

A successful investor is a person who has deep knowledge of timing of macro and micro market which allows him to earn handsome profits in investment.

In India, property cycle usually remains stable. It increases slowly. A professional investor should exit from the cycle as soon as he gets a good price. How long do you keep a property after purchasing is not as important as purchasing a good property with saleable attributes like a good location, good construction quality, ample amenities, transport connectivity and other facilities.

Generally, a person should hold the investment at least for 3 years to account for the capital gain. If you have taken a housing loan from a bank, always consider the income tax issue and take the advantage of 80C. Suppose you have decided to sell the property within five years. Then the whole income tax benefit availed by you from principal payment would be reverted. The exempt principal amount will be clubbed in your income in that financial year and you have to pay tax on it. So normally hold the investment for at least five years if you are availing principal payment benefit for home loan.

Consider prepayment charges on loan if applicable. These days banks are not charging prepayment charges after the introduction of the National Housing Board Guidelines. Also consider rental income obtained during investment period. Decorate the property before you sell it as well as consider other charges like brokerage fee. Normally property broker charges 1 to 2 % of sale consideration.

There are three basic reasons to sell a property

1. If property was purchased for investment.
2. A growing family or an enhancement in your status or financial status may prompt you to upgrade your residential

house property. At that time you may have to sell your current residential property. However, doing so, do keep in mind the aspects connected with the income-tax and, the stamp duty payment before taking such decisions.

If you are selling your property due to any of the reasons mentioned above, then you should sell the property when market is high.

3. When a person needs funds in emergencies like illness, marriage, business need or deficit then he has to sell his property immediately.

Whenever you decide to sell your property you should take following steps to get the best price.

1. **Vacate The House/Flat First:** The reason is that an occupied house seems 25 to 40% smaller than a vacant house. If house/flat is occupied, the purchaser will not be able to understand the actual space available in the house. A vacant house may help the buyer to make the decision faster because he can then visualize himself living in it. When you are offering your house for sale, the buyers may come at any time to visit the house. It may hamper your privacy. There are chances that some unscrupulous characters may also visit your house. This may put you and your family in danger. Keep the house vacant; provide one key to broker and other key in your possession.
2. **Decorate The House:** Before selling the house decorate it well. Whitewash the house and color the doors and windows. Repair all fittings. If there is any leakage or breakage in house then get it repaired. It makes a good impression on buyers. Always remember that first impression is last impression. Doing up the house many help you to increase the selling price by 10 - 20%. However, for this you will only have to spend 0.1% to 1% of cost of house property. Change the

interior as well as exterior of the house. If flooring is old you may also change it.

3. **Prepare a list of the unique selling points and features of the house:** How much rent will you get? What is so special about your house? For example, is it well ventilated, east facing, lucky for your family, etc? What are the amenities, which are available near to your house like market, hospital, school, and park? When you decide to sell your house, it is you who has to act as the brand ambassador of your house and do the marketing.

4. **Always Keep a Photocopy of Chain of Documents With You:** The buyer should never be given a chance to re-think his decision. Your documents should be ready and you should be able to ensure a smooth and easy transaction. If you have taken loan from bank then always obtain list of property documents which are deposited by you in bank as security.

5. **Make the Deal Attractive:** You may make the deal even more attractive by offering the buyer a window of two months to pay the entire money. In case of a good deal, you can offer to bear the legal charges.

6. **Don't Disclose the Real Reason For Sale:** Buyer will always be eager to know that why are you selling the property. Never let him know the true reason for the sale. For example, if you are selling because of a problem or cash crunch, don't let the buyer know that because then he will try to negotiate and you will lose the upper hand. Instead give him reasons like you'd like to purchase a bigger house or you are moving to a different city.

7. **Always Decide Fair Value:** Before you decide to sell your property, first find out market rates near your property. Try to contact some brokers and ask them the market price of

the houses in that particular area. Also keep in mind location of your house like corner plot, park facing, east facing, road size on which it is located like 30 feet road or 60 feet road. Now tell the buyer a fair value which is not hypothecated. Tell the purchaser that he is going to purchase the best property for which the price will be appreciable in the near future.

8. **Ask the Buyer Regarding The Arrangement of Funds For Deal:** Sometimes, a property purchaser unwillingly gets stuck in a deal due to poor CIBIL scores. When you are going to sell a property and are almost going to finalize the deal, always advise a potential buyer to get his provisional loan sanctioned before doing the agreement to sale. There is possibility that the bank backs out at a late stage due to poor credit history of buyer.

❑

34

Pradhan Mantri Awas Yojana (PMAY)

"Housing for All" Mission for urban areas is being implemented by Govt. of India, Ministry of Housing and Urban Poverty Alleviation with effect from 17.06.2015 to provide central assistance to implementing agencies. The Credit Linked Subsidy Scheme is being offered under this mission.

PMAY (Urban) Mission was launched on 25th June 2015 which intends to provide "Housing for All" by 31st March 2022, the 150th birth anniversary year of Mahatma Gandhi, by constructing 20 million houses across the nation.

The Mission provides Central Assistance to the implementing agencies through States/Union Territories (UTs) and Central Nodal Agencies (CNAs) for providing houses to all eligible families/ beneficiaries against the validated demand for houses for about 1.12 cr.

For Middle Income Group (MIG), the interest subsidy will be provided on housing loans for acquisition/construction of houses (including purchase) up to 31st March 2021.

For Economically Weaker Section (EWS)/Lower Income Group (LIG), the interest subsidy will be provided on housing loans for acquisition, construction of house. The Credit Linked subsidy would also be available for home loan availed for new construction and addition of rooms, kitchen, toilet etc. to existing dwellings as incremental housing. The interest subsidy benefit will be upfront on principal outstanding. The availability and amount of interest subsidy is subject to meeting income criteria as per various categories under the scheme.

At present, the PMAY (Urban) has around 4,331 such towns and cities under this scheme. It also includes urban development authority, special area development authority, industrial development authority, development area, notified planning, and every other authority which is responsible for urban planning and regulation.

Beneficiary

- A beneficiary family will comprise of husband, wife, unmarried sons and/or unmarried daughters.
- An adult earning member (irrespective of marital status) can be treated as a separate household.

Beneficiaries can avail the benefits of this scheme by meeting the following few eligibility criteria –

- He/she must not own a house to fulfill the Pradhan Mantri Awas Yojana eligibility.
- The individual must also not avail the benefits of any other housing scheme by the State or Central Government.

Key Parameters*

Particulars	EWS	LIG	MIG I	MIG II
Household Income (Rs. p.a)	0-3,00,000	3,00,001-6,00,000	6,00,001-12,00,000	12,00,001-18,00,000
Eligible Housing Loan Amount for Interest Subsidy (₹)	Up to 6,00,000	Up to 6,00,000	Up to 9,00,000	Up to 12,00,000
Interest Subsidy (% p.a.)	6.50%	6.50%	4.00%	3.00%

Maximum loan tenure (in years)	20	20	20	20
Maximum dwelling unit carpet area	30 Sq. m.	60 Sq. m.	160 Sq. m.	200 Sq. m.
Discount Rate for Net Present Value (NPV) calculation of interest subsidy (%)	9.00%	9.00%	9.00%	9.00%
Max. Interest Subsidy Amount (Rs.)	2,67,280	2,67,280	2,35,068	2,30,156
Application of scheme on existing home loans sanctioned on or after	17.06.2015		01.01.2017	
Applicability of No Pucca House	Not for renovation/up gradation		Yes	Yes
Woman Ownership/ Co-ownership	Mandatory for new acquisition, Not mandatory for existing property		Not mandatory	Not mandatory

* Economically Weaker Section (EWS), Low Income Group (LIG)

* Middle Income Group I (MIG I), Middle Income Group II (MIG II)

Home loans under the CLSS have a maximum tenor of 20 years. NPV or the net present value is evaluated at a discounted rate of 9% of the interest subsidy.

Beneficiaries can apply for PMAY through the following:

A. **Online:** Individuals can visit the official website of the scheme to apply online. They need to have a valid Aadhaar Card to apply.

B. **Offline:** Beneficiaries can apply for the scheme offline by filling up a form available through Common Service Centre (CSC). Price of these forms is ₹25 + GST.

❑

35

Capital Gain in Real Estate

What is Capital Gain?

When a property is sold, a word called 'Capital Gain' is often used. It is a word that makes a person happy with a little tension. Any profits or gains arising from the transfer of a capital asset effected in the previous year, shall be chargeable to income tax under the head Capital Gains and shall be deemed to be the income of the previous year in which the transfer took place unless such capital gain is exempt u/s 54, 54B, 54D, 54EC, 54F, 54G, 54GA or 54GB.Capital gains are basically of two types, one is short term capital gain and another is long term capital gain.

- **Capital Asset:** Capital Asset plays an important role in Capital Gain. As per Section 2(14) of the Income-tax Act, 1961 defines the term capital asset as property of any kind held by an assessee, whether or not connected with his business or profession, but does not include certain items like consumable store, stock-in-trade or raw materials held for the purpose of his own business or profession, personal effects and certain agricultural lands. However, jewelry held for personal use would be subjected to capital gains. Thus, house building, flat, penthouse, farmhouse, shops/ showroom and also land would all fall within the definition of capital assets.

- **Transfer of Capital Asset:** Capital gain arises only when there is a transfer of capital asset. Transfer includes sale, exchange, relinquishment of the asset and the transfer for the purpose of capital gains means change in ownership of capital asset. Section 5 of the Transfer of Property Act, 1882 provides that transfer of property means an act by which a living person conveys property in present or in future, to one or more other living persons. To transfer property is to perform sucha an act. If the sale price is the market rate then sale consideration would be considered for stamp duty as well for capital gain purpose. If sale consideration is less than circle rate then the circle rate of the property sold shall be treated as the deemed sale price. It is mentioned clear cut in Section 50C of the Income-tax Act, 1961 that the value of a transaction as adopted for the purposes of stamp duty would be the value treated as deemed sale consideration of the property for the purpose of calculation of the capital gains payable by an assessee. In case the assessee claims before the Assessing Officer that the value assessed or adopted by the Stamp Valuation Authority or Sub Registrar Office exceeds the fair market value of the property as on the sale deed execution in that situation the Assessing Officer may refer the valuation of the property to a Valuation Officer. For all practical purposes, transfer would mean the date on which possession has been given of the immovable property. If there is agreement to sale between two parties and payment has been received by seller but transfer has not been affected or sale deed not executed, then it would not be treated as a sale transaction. It is clear in the income tax rule that income-tax would be chargeable under the head capital gains only if there is a transfer of a capital asset during the previous year. No transfer means no capital gain.

- **Short Term Capital Gain:** If the immovable property is sold by the owner within 36 months from the date of purchase then the income would be treated as a short term capital gain. However, there is no possibility of tax saving with reference to short-term capital gain. The tax liability of short-term capital gain would be calculated by adding the amount of the short-term capital gain with the other taxable income of the year and thereafter calculating the tax liability as per the tax rates on the total income.

- **Long Term Capital Gain:** If a property is held more than 36 months from the date of purchase or sale deed, then the capital gain arising thereon is treated as long-term capital gain. Long term capital gains are charged tax @ 20 per cent. The amount of capital gains is arrived at by applying concept of Cost Inflation Index.

  It means the period of holding the asset from the date of purchase till the date of sale, is the main factor to determine whether it is short term capital gain or long term capital gain.

- **Capital Gain Bonds:** These are financial instruments especially designated for the investors who have long term capital gain tax liability. These bonds are basically of two types and are issued by REC, PFC & NHAI. No other bonds qualify in this category. It is possible for all categories of investors to completely set off their capital gains tax liability by investing in capital gains bonds in terms of section 54EC of the Income-tax Act, 1961. Investment of the net long-term capital gain in the acquisition of bonds within six months of sale of property and to be retained for a minimum period of five years w.e.f. 01.04.2020. The maximum amount which can be invested in these bonds is ₹50 lakh during the financial year. If a property is jointly held by two brothers and they earn capital gain of ₹100 lakh from selling of it then each of them would be eligible for investment of ₹50 lakh in capital gain bonds. It means that the amount of money invested by a taxpayer is limited.

- In the alternative, individual/HUF might also invest in residential house property in certain circumstances to save the liability of capital gains tax. The capital loss of both short term or long term, can be carried forward and set off for the next 8 years.

Capital Gains Tax

As the name indicates, tax which is payable on capital gain is known as capital gain tax. Long term capital gains are charged to tax @ 20 percent. Long term capital gains may be derived from selling of residential property or plot or any other assets.

According to Section 54F of the Income Tax Act, 1961, if a person sells capital assets other than residential house, he can save capital gain tax by investing entire net sale consideration in a new residential house.

According to Section 54 of the Income Tax Act, 1961, if a person sells a residential house, he can save capital gain tax by investing net consideration or capital gain in a new residential house with fulfilling certain conditions which are mentioned in the law.

One of the conditions is that, the new residential property purchased or constructed is not transferred within a period of 3 years from the date of acquisition If the new property is sold within a period of 3 years from the date of its acquisition, then, for the purpose of computing the capital gains on this transfer, the cost of acquisition of this house property shall be reduced by the amount of capital gain exempt under section 54 earlier. The capital gain arising from this transfer will always be a short term capital gain.

Mr. Chidrup Jain was an owner of a residential house situated in Goa sold his property on 2nd April 2020. He had a capital gain of ₹15 lakh. Now to save tax on capital gain, he has planned to purchase a new residential property (house/flat) within stipulated time i.e. up to due date of ITR filling (Probably 31st July 2021). If he is unable to purchase the property on due date of filling then he has to shift the capital gain amount to Capital Gain Account Scheme. Now he has a question in mind, in whose name he should purchase the new property? Friends, in this situation you should follow Section 54 of the Income Tax Act, 1961 which clearly states that if Mr. X wants to save capital gains tax, he should always purchase property in his name only. If he purchases property in his wife or other relative names then he would not be eligible for saving tax on capital gain. Don't forget this fact. This principle is also applicable if you want to construct the residential house on a plot which is in your name only or you are contemplating to purchase a vacant plot and construct thereon.

Mr. Rajeev Tyagi was allotted a plot from Rajasthan Housing Board in year 2008. In year 2013 he sold the plot to Mr. Narsi Lal. Now he has a capital gain of ₹30 lakhs. However, the benefit of interest on borrowed funds for investment in a vacant land can be availed by him while calculating the taxable capital gain.

Now he has three options:

1. Pay capital gain tax @ 20 % of net consideration or capital gain. He has to pay ₹6 lakhs as capital gain tax.
2. If he wants to save tax on capital gain on the sale of the vacant plot of land after three years, then he has to think

about investment of the net consideration in the acquisition of bonds to be retained for a minimum period of five years. Only three types of bonds (issued by REC, PFC & NHAI) qualify for this exemption under the provisions of Section 54EC of the Income tax Act. He has to purchase a bond of ₹30 lakh.

3. The third and last option which is to obtain full (100%) exemption from long term capital gain is to use the entire sale proceeds of the vacant plot within three years to construct a residential house property either for one's own self occupation purposes or for letting the same out to tenants. Further Rajeev (seller or assessee), can use the entire sale proceeds in the purchasing of a house/flat within two years from the date of sale and claim full exemption thereof under the provisions of section 54F of the Income-tax Act, 1961. If he has already purchased a new house one year before from date of selling of the old house then he can adjust his entire sale consideration to save capital gain. However, remember that duration should be only one year.

   Mr. Rajeev is a wise man he did all calculations properly. His children have completed college education and are now settled. He paid capital gain tax as even after that he has a huge amount in bank account. If he creates a fix deposit of whole amount in his name then he has to pay more tax on total income, since he is in the 30% slab of income tax. He gifted ₹10 lakh to each of his sons who are in the lower tax slab. Thus, he has done proper financial planning. Friends, remember that capital gain bonds are suitable for those persons who don't want to take any risk in life. If you are capable of generating return @ 12 to 15 % by investing it in real estate, business and share market then don't invest in capital bonds.

From the Assessment Year 1999-2000 HUF and all individuals are eligible for complete exemption not only in respect of one residential house property for their own use but also for a vacant plot having area up to 500 sq. meters under the provisions of Section 5 (vi) of the Wealth Tax Act, 1957.

Cost Inflation Index (CII)

You can save a sufficient amount of tax on long-term capital gain by using the cost inflation index. This index is applicable only on long-term capital gain not for short-term capital gain.

How it is calculated? There is a set formula which is to be used for calculation of long-term capital gain.

First of all, find out financial year in which the house was purchased. Write down the cost of purchasing/acquisition (purchasing price including registration charge and brokerage charge) and cost of inflation index for that year. Now write down the cost of inflation index of the financial year in which asset was sold. Now, the cost of acquisition of the asset is to be multiplied by the cost inflation index of that year in which the asset is transferred/sold and the resulting figure is to be divided by the cost-inflation index for the year in which the asset was purchased or acquired. If a house property was purchased before 01/04/2001 then the fair market value of property as on 01/04/2001 would be considered as acquisition cost of property and the cost inflation index for the asset would be considered the cost inflation index of 2001-02 or it should be considered that it was purchased on 1st April 2001.

Illustration:

Mr. Satya Prakash Singh purchased property for ₹50,00,000 in the year 2001-02. He sold it on 1st May 2019 for ₹1, 50, 00,000. The long term capital gain would be calculated as under:

Cost of acquisition for the purpose of capital gains

= (Cost of acquisition × Cost inflation index of the year of transfer)/ (Cost Inflation Index of the year in which purchased)

= (50,00,000 × 289/100 = ₹1,44,50,000)

(CII for F.Y. 2019-20 is 289 and for F.Y. 2001-02 is 100)

Sale Price = ₹150,00,000

Less:

Adjusted cost price taking into 1,44,50,000 account the impact of cost inflation index LTC gains = ₹5,50,000/.

* Sometimes people purchase a society land and after a period of two to ten years or even more, local development authority or Nagar Nigam organizes a camp. They ask the people to deposit lease money and registration charge, after which they issue Patta/Lease Deed for 99 years in favor of land owner. It means any cost incurred to get the clear title (lease money, stamp duty and registration charge) or also brokerage charge (up to 1% of purchase price) are to be similarly adjusted with the help of the cost inflation index, i.e. by multiplying the cost of incurred clear title by the cost inflation index of the year in which the asset was sold and be divided by the cost inflation index for the year in which the asset was registered.

* Sometimes you purchase a plot and later on construct a house on it. Or sometime you purchase a single storey house and later on construct another storey. It means any cost incurred on the improvement of an asset is to be similarly adjusted with the help of cost inflation index, i.e. by multiplying the cost of improvement by the cost inflation index of the year in which the asset is transferred, and be divided by the cost inflation index for the year in which the improvement/construction to the asset was done.

The Government of India notifies the yearly cost inflation index for every financial year.

Following is the Cost inflation index chart from 2001-02 to 2019-20

Financial Year	Cost inflation index	Financial Year	Cost inflation index
0000-0000	000	2010-2011	167
2001-2002	100	2011-2012	184
2002-2003	105	2012-2013	200
2003-2004	109	2013-2014	220
2004-2005	113	2014-2015	240

2005-2006	117	2015-2016	254
2006-2007	122	2016-2017	264
2007-2008	129	2017-2018	272
2008-2009	137	2018-2019	280
2009-2010	148	2019-2020	289

Illustration:

Mr. Yogesh Shroti purchased a house for 1,09,000 on 15/11/2005 and paid ₹10000 for registration charge in the office of sub registrar to get the house registered in his name. ₹1000 was paid as brokerage charge to property dealer on purchase date. On 06th May 2015 he spent ₹1,00,000 on improvement of the house. The house was sold on 30th March 2018 for ₹1500000. Commission of ₹15000 (1% of sale price) was paid to property dealer. Compute the capital gain.

Sale Price or sale consideration =.......................₹15, 00,000

Less:

1. Expenses on sale/transfer...................................₹15000
2. Indexed cost of acquisition 120000 X 272/117 =........₹2,78,974
3. Indexed cost of improvement 100000 X 272/254 = ₹1,07,087

Long Term Capital Gain...................................... ₹10,98,939

Expense on registration and brokerage are part of acquisition so the total cost of acquisition will be Rs 1,20,000 [purchase price (109000) + registration charges (10000) + brokerage charges (1000)]

*Net sale consideration will be 1500000-15000 = ₹ 1485000.

Illustration:

Mr. X purchased property on 01/09/2002 for ₹500,000 and paid ₹20000 for registration charges. Mr. X died on 15/11/2008 and property was transferred to his son Mr. Y through inheritance. Market value of property on 15/11/2008 was ₹18,00,000.

Mr. Y sold the property on 21/07/2019 for ₹30,00,000. Compute the long term capital gain or loss for Financial Year 2019-20 (Assessment Year 2020-21).

Sale Price or sale consideration = ₹30,00,000

Less:

1. Indexed cost of acquisition* 520000 × 289/105 =... ₹14,31,238

Long Term Capital Gain...................................... ₹ 15,68,762/-

* Expenses occurred at the time of acquisition of property will be added in purchasing price like registry charges and brokerage charges so acquisition cost will be ₹ 520000.

*Index cost of acquisition =Cost of acquisition to the previous owner (Purchase price for Mr. X) X CII of the year of transfer)/CII of the year in which the asset is first held by the assessee.

Illustration:

Mr. Mantosh purchased property for ₹20,00,000 in the year 2001-02. He sold this in the financial year 2019-2020 for ₹48, 50,000. The long-term capital gain would be calculated as under:

Sale Price or sale consideration = ₹48,50,000

Less:

Indexed cost of acquisition 20,00,000 X289/100 = ₹57, 80,000

Long Term Capital Loss.............................₹ 9,30,000/

In this case, the selling price is lower than the cost of acquisition as computed with reference to the cost inflation index (₹ 57,80,000).

Hence, there will be no capital gains tax payable, rather, there will be a long-term capital loss to the tune of ₹9,30,000 which can be carried forward for adjustment against Mantosh's total long-term capital gains.

Sometime you take a home loan for purchasing a residential property and take benefit of section 80C and 24. During the tenure of loan you pay EMI having interest component. When you sell the property, you may have a question in mind that can you club your interest portion in the cost of acquisition. Dear friends, you cannot do this because you have already taken the benefit of the interest of loan under section 24 of income tax. So, home loan interest payment has no role in capital gain tax. You should remember that the benefit of cost inflation index is not available for short-term capital gains or losses. Thus, selling residential property within a period of less than three years from the date of its purchases is considered as a short-term capital gain or loss in respect of gain from property. Further, the benefit of the cost inflation index is not available to non-resident Indians.

Mr. Bajrang Lal Kumawat purchased property on 11th March, 2018 and sold the same on 25/11/2018. The Purchase price was ₹15 lakh and the sale price ₹18 lakh, thus the profit is Rs3 lakh. As this is a short-term capital gain, the benefit of cost inflation index is not available. So ₹3.00 lakh would be added to Mr. Bajrang's income and he is liable to pay tax at the normal rate.

Capital Gain Accounts Scheme

On 22nd June 1988, the Government of India launched a popular scheme known as Capital Gain Accounts Scheme for the benefit of the people who derive only and only long-term capital gain. Individual, NRI, Proprietorship Firm, HUF can also take benefit from this scheme. This scheme is not beneficial for short term capital gain.

The scheme is beneficial for the people who have derived long term capital gain and now want to purchase a property within two years or construct a house within three years from the date of sale to save long term capital gain tax.

Dear friends, to save tax on capital gain there are various provisions in the Income-tax Act, 1961. One of them is that the investment should be made in acquiring new residential property within 2 years from the date of sale or constructing a house within 3 years from the date of sale.

Illustration:

Mr. X has sold his residential property on 2nd April 2018. Now if he wants to take benefit of this scheme, he has to purchase a new residential property within two years from the sale. According to this example on or before 1st April 2020, or and if Mr. X already has a plot and he wants to construct a house on that plot then his construction work should be completed (within three years) on or before 1st April 2021. But after selling his property Mr. X has not decided which property to purchase or whether to should start a constructing on the plot or not. It means he is unable to take the decision to make the investment in residential property by the last date of filing the income-tax return which is 31st July, 2019 in this case. In this situation, he should open a Capital Gain Account at a designated Bank and the amount must be deposited on or before 31st July, 2019. If he will sell his property on 31st March, 2019 then he has to open account on or before 31st July, 2019.The reason is that for the financial year 2018-19 (in which property is to be sold), the last date of filing ITR is 31st July, 2019.

The Capital Gain Account should be open in only authorized banks and rural branches of these designated banks are not permitted to open Capital Gain Account.

The Government has identified some banks to accept the deposit under Capital Gain Accounts Scheme 1988. The banks which accept capital gain deposit are SBI, PNB, Bank of Baroda, Bank Of India, Canara Bank, Union Bank Of India, Central Bank of India, UCO Bank, Indian Bank, Bank of Maharashtra and Punjab & Sind Bank. Other than the above no other bank is authorized to accept the deposit under Capital Gain Accounts Scheme.

Two types of deposit accounts are available. The first account is known as Deposit Saving Account A wherein the deposit shall be in the form of saving deposit. Passbook is issued by bank. Term Deposit Account B, has an option to retain the deposit either as "cumulative" (with interest reinvested) also known as DRC (Deposit Reinvestment Receipt) or as Noncumulative (interest shift to saving account). Such deposits may be made as a single lump-sum amount or in installment at any time on or before furnishing the income tax return. Initially, a person who wants to open capital gain account is allowed to open only type A account. After that he is permitted to open type B account.

Friends, remember that you should open only capital gain account by filling form-A. Confirm from bank officer that it is a capital gain account that you are opting for. Otherwise you may have problems in future. A majority of people in India open a normal savings account to save capital gain. Remember, the income tax department is quite strict about this.

Withdrawals under Deposit account 'A' can be made from time to time by the depositor. Normally to transfer from Type 'A' deposit to type B, a term deposit is created but on maturity or prematurity they are transferred to Type 'A' deposit Account. For nomination facility form –E is required. Depositor has to fill up Form C if he requires money to be withdrawn for the purposes of making payment for the residential property. You should remember that withdrawal amount should be used within 60 days from the date of withdrawal for construction or purchase of property.

If depositor withdraws money for purchasing new property and the deal is cancelled due to some reason or there is a delay in finalizing the deal, he can deposit the withdrawn amount in account A within 60 days of the withdrawal. Depositor intending to make withdrawal from his account –B shall first get the amount transferred to his account –A, and then may withdraw the amount in the same manner as from A. The withdrawal for more than ₹25000/- will be allowed through cross demand draft in favor of the person to whom the depositor wants to make payment. Form –D in duplicate is to be used for all subsequent withdrawals after initial withdrawal.

❑

36

Role of Second House for You

If you have more than one residential house, it shows that you are financially sound and prosperous. Friends, for proper real estate planning each member of family should have separate property in his or her name. Remember in the absence of advance planning, second house property in your name may cause a problem to you from tax point of view. Hence, avoid purchasing second house property in your name only. Let other family members also get a chance to become proud owners of their own property. Otherwise you may have problems. Some families purchase property in the name of HUF to avoid this situation.

As you know that first/one house property is completely exempt from wealth tax. For one property, wealth tax exemption is related neither from its size nor its value. The second residential house property would, however, be subjected to wealth tax.

Another disadvantage of having a second property in your name is also related to 80C and 24 of income tax act 1961. In case of a self-occupied house you will not be able to save the tax on the interest component of the loan. The Income Tax Law very clearly states that home loan taken on or after 1st April, 1999 in respect of a residential house or flat deduction under Section 24 in respect of interest on loan that would be allowed to a limit of ₹2,00,000 p.a. However, if a person purchases a second house property or constructs a second house on a vacant plot with help of a housing loan for his self-occupation then he is not eligible to take benefit of deduction of interest component of the loan since section 24 of income tax allows a deduction only in respect of one residential self-occupied house property.

Another important limitation of purchasing a second residential house property in your name is that the second house occupied by you is supposed to generate income which is called as deemed income. Hence, this clause attracts additional tax even if you are not earning any income from the second house. The Income tax law clearly states that your first house property has nil income. But the second and subsequent, residential house properties which are kept for own use would be subjected to income tax in respect of deemed rental income. So always purchase the second and subsequent houses for investment purposes or letting it out. So, smart real estate financial planning would be where each family member can be an owner of one self-occupied residential house property and benefit from wealth tax exemptions well as enjoy the benefit of deduction in respect of interest on loan for one residential house property.

After about fifteen years, it is wise to start looking for your second house. That way you would have a new house to move into after twenty years which is the ideal life cycle of a house or apartment these days.

❑

37

Senior Citizen Homes

In the twenty first century the increase in the average life expectancy due to better medical facilities coupled with the degeneration of joint family concept has made senior citizens quite vulnerable in their final years of life.

Old people require their own township for their care and welfare. Today's retirement homes take care of all the needs of senior citizens, and do it in style.

Private developers are taking interest in this field. As more affluent Indians join the ranks of retirees, the demand for housing projects catering exclusively to this category is on the rise. There are at least 30 such projects and an equal number is on the drawing board. Most of these retirement homes are located in the suburbs of metros, but some are being developed at well-known retirement destinations, such as Coimbatore, Goa and Dehradun.

Don't consider these housing projects like old-age homes, where the aged and abandoned live in a pitiable state. Today's retirement homes are vibrant townships that take care of food, housekeeping, health care and security, allowing senior citizens to enjoy their sunset years.

What are the Reasons For Growing Demand?

Several factors are driving the demand for retirement homes in India. India's so-called demographic dividend will soon turn grey. India is a country of youth and there are 60 million (roughly 8% of the Indian population) people over 60 years of age in India and this count is expected to double by year 2030. The country's overall population is growing at 1.8% annually, but the ranks of senior citizens are swelling at a much faster rate of 3.8% every year. Considering this scenario, several large corporate groups, such as the Ashiana Group (Utsav), LIC Housing Finance Limited (LIC HFL Care Homes), Tata Housing Development Company Limited (Tata Riva at Bangalore) and Max India Limited (Antara Senior Living in Dehradun) have entered in the arena of constructing of homes for senior citizens.

The present demand for retirement housing in India is approximately 3 lakh units. There's an option to suit every pocket, with unit sizes varying from 300 sq ft to 2500 sq ft. A basic apartment costs up to ₹25 - 30 lakh, while a mid-sized unit can cost ₹55-65 Lakh. It also varies from city to city and location to location. For those with deep pockets, there are luxury villas with price tags of ₹1 crore and above. Apart from this, there are separate charges for the services offered. The monthly charges for a couple can be approximated to ₹5,000-25,000 for standard services, and ₹30, 000-50,000 for luxury services

Many senior citizens are financially independent and have full support from their families when they retire. However, the problem arises when their grown-up children move to another city, or country, for work. Safety concerns, healthcare needs and loneliness/isolation are pushing these people to opt for retirement resorts that offer convenient solutions to these problems.

Safety, Security and Health Care Are Areas of Concern

Safety and security are important concerns, especially because of the rise in crime against senior citizens in cities. Many assisted-living centers provide 24- hour security as well as CCTV facility for their senior citizens to make sure that all is well. There is also the provision of emergency healthcare services. If there is an accident or some medical emergency, the senior citizen can be quickly taken to a hospital or given first aid. Such an assurance is also a big relief for their children, who may have moved to another city or country for work.

What Precaution should be kept in Mind before you opt for it?

First of all, inspect the project where you are going to invest and ask people about facility provider (township developer or group) whether the facilities being provided match with the price charged. If the services have been outsourced, then check out the reputation of the service provider. Also check whether the services provided are as per the expectations of the residents. In case this is a new project, then ask people living in other such projects developed by the same developer. If possible, visit the company's older projects and enquire from residents how satisfied they are. In particular, find out about the service provider's level of specialization in geriatric care. These projects offer a number of facilities, but they come at a premium compared to regular housing projects. Instead of focusing on the luxury aspects and premium fittings, you need to make sure that the project is well connected with rail and road and offers all essential amenities within the campus.

Do every calculation while buying a house in a project. The cost of the services will rise every year. Since you will be living off your savings, don't over-extend and buy into a project you can't afford.

Three Ways to buy a Retirement Home

Senior housing projects are tailored to the needs of the aged. One can choose from any of the three financial models on offer.

Outright Sale

Ashiana Housing and Tata Group are providing such types of senior citizen homes. This is similar to a normal sale proceeding. The flats/villas in retirement projects are sold to customers above the age of 50 or 55 on a per sq ft basis. The whole project is maintained by professionally qualified persons. Here services are offered on a monthly payment plan. Children of these residents cannot live with their parents. They can stay for a short period. A son or daughter, whose age is less than 50 years, can also buy such a unit, but only a senior citizen is allowed to stay permanently in the society.

Deposit Model/Payback Schemes

An upfront deposit which is a percentage (60-70 %) of the sale value of the unit is charged according to the size of the unit. This includes residential charges only. Charges are levied as actual for food, electricity, water, etc. The deposit charges are paid back to the successor with some deductions for administration/ cancellation charges.

Lifetime Lease

A small deposit is charged on handing over the unit to the customer. A recurring monthly rent is levied for the duration of stay (this includes rent, electricity and water charges). The rest of the facilities (food, health care, security and social engagements) are paid as per actual basis. One benefit of this option is that the unit holder doesn't have to pay property tax.

Enjoy life!

When a person becomes old, his health and physical condition push him into depression. Living in a residential complex, where neighbors are in constant touch, can be uplifting. The residents in a retirement complex may not exactly be family, but they provide the much-needed companionship that seniors are looking for. The opportunity to interact and enjoy together improves the quality of life. We see a growing need for assisted living centers in the country due to the changing demographics, migration of children for work, breaking down of the joint family system, and difficulty in managing by oneself in cities.

In the past, there was a social stigma attached to abandoning one's parents in a retirement home. However, attitudes have changed over the years. Though this concept is still in a nascent stage, at least it is not looked down upon anymore.

A considerable portion of the demand for luxury retirement homes is from non-resident Indians (NRIs). Senior NRIs accustomed to top-end facilities in developed countries and returning to their home country, or those whose children have turned NRIs, are significant potential customers.

Is It A Sound Investment?

Is it a wise decision to invest in retirement home? Dear friends, these houses are bought primarily for end users for their own residential needs after retirement. So never choose them as investment tool. Always focus on the benefits you are likely to derive from them, not so much on their price appreciation.

As you know that profit from investment is dependent on demand and supply curve. Whether you or your heirs get price appreciation from the house will depend on demand and supply. Nowadays there is a limited supply of senior citizen housing projects, even with the rising demand. If this continues, you may earn good returns. However, if supply increases, the returns may not be so good.

An important consideration to look at in case of these projects is that generally banks do not finance these projects.

This is because in case of defaulters, bank cannot sell it to a person who is below 50 years. This restriction prevents bank from financing retirement homes. In India, most people want to bequeath a house to their children. If you buy a retirement home, you can pass it on to your children, but they will not be able to live there till they are of a certain age (usually 50 or 55). This is one factor that works against the popularity of retirement homes and the investment return from retirement homes is lower than that from normal residential houses. Builders are developing these projects in the outskirts of the city because the land is available at lower price, which helps in keeping the cost of these houses low.

Always choose the rent option for some time before you take the plunge. You may not like the lifestyle or other features or may not be used to living in such a set-up. It may even make sense to live on rent forever. This is the best model from the point of view of flexibility. You also get to keep your capital and can use it to generate a cash flow. If the service provider does not deliver, you have the option to exit. Ashiana Utsav at Lavasa has created a novel concept of Trial Homes to give a firsthand experience of the life at retirement homes. In this, a new customer can experience the living conditions and ambience of Senior Citizen Homes before they decide to permanently join the community. A Trial Home is a fully furnished 2BHK apartment equipped with all the facilities for a comfortable and peaceful stay of visitors or prospective buyers.

Assess your Needs and then Take a Decision for Shifting

Your choice will also depend on the level of care you need. This progressively changes as you grow older. Most of the retirement homes that are coming up cater only to those in sound health. There are some who cater to those who can manage most of their tasks, but need help with a few chores. However, there is very little choice for individual who needs help with all activities. At that stage, one may need full-time care, which comes at a very high cost.

Another question that needs to be answered is what do you plan to do with your own house, which is in the same city where retirement home is situated? It could fetch you enough money to buy the retirement apartment and live comfortably for the rest of your life house after you move into a retirement home. However, that also means that you will have no back-up options. What if you don't like the life away from the city in which you have lived in for 50-60 years? What if you miss your friends and family?

Some people who have used their life time saving to purchase a retirement homes retain their houses in the city. This can lead to a situation where the person has two assets but does not have enough cash. He may be an owner of a house worth ₹10 million in the market, but won't have enough to pay for his medical bills or buy groceries. At this time, reverse mortgage may be the good option. Another problem that arises is that retirement home is not as liquid as other real estate options. Banks and housing finance companies are not as willing to extend loans because the buyer's income has come down after retirement. So the decision to shift in a retirement home is not something that you can take lightly. Weigh the pros and cons, conduct thorough research, and only then make the move.

❑

38

Reverse Mortgage Loan

In keeping up their role of meeting the aspirations of all sections of society at different stages of life, banks have a product named as "Reverse Mortgage Loan" catering to the financial needs of senior citizens.

Old age comes with its own share of problems. As a person grows older, and his regular source of income dries up, his dependency on others can increase significantly. With health care expenses on the rise and little social security, living the golden years respectfully can be quite a challenge for senior citizens. In such condition, a regular income stream that can help them to meet their financial needs and maintain their current living standards becomes important.

This loan provides a source of additional income for senior citizens, who own self-occupied and self-acquired house property in India. The property against which the senior citizen proposes to raise the loan should be his permanent primary residence. Residual life of property should be at least 20 years. Loan amount should not be used for speculative, trading and business purposes.

The amount received through reverse mortgage is considered as a loan, not income, so it will not attract any tax liability.

Reverse Mortgage Loan encompasses a range of non-recourse mortgage loans which help senior citizens to get regular liquid funds against his/her home equity, without having to move out or having to make any repayments till he / she dies or sells the house. Since bulk of the savings at retirement is typically locked in home equity, Reverse Mortgage is a powerful device to increase the incomes in old age.

One typical feature with most senior citizens is that their residential property accounts for a significant portion of their total asset pie, and given its nature, property fails to aid senior citizens on the liquidity front. In the reverse mortgage, senior citizens who own a house property but do not have a regular income can mortgage the same with the lender (a scheduled bank or a housing finance company). In return, the lender makes monthly payments to the borrowers during their lifetime subject to a maximum period of 20 years. The loan amount along with future interest will be 70% to 90 % of the assessed market value of the property (according to location of property, like metro area or urban area) subject to maximum of ₹100 lakh. Payment is credited in the saving account of the borrower.

In spite of mortgaging the house property, the borrower and spouse can continue to stay in it during their entire life span and continue to receive regular flow of income from the lender as well. Also, since the borrower does not have to service the loan, he need not bother about repaying the 'borrowed amount' to the lender. The lender will recover the loan along with the accumulated interest by selling the house after the death of the borrower or earlier, if the borrower leaves the mortgaged residential property permanently to an institution or to relatives.

Senior citizens are an increasing component of Indian society and dependency in old age is increasing in our country. Increase in average life expectancy because of better medical facilities coupled with the degeneration of joint family concept has made them vulnerable in their final years of life. Senior citizens need a regular additional source of cash flow to augment their pension/ other income. As a major chunk of senior citizen's investment lies in home equity, reverse mortgage can be very effective in ensuring a steady and precious income in the old age.

Loan can be taken singly or jointly with spouse in case of a living spouse, the minimum age of first borrower should be 60 years and spouse should be 55 years and above. But number of surviving members should not be more than one spouse.

The loan shall become due and payable only when the last surviving borrower dies or opts to sell the home, or permanently moves out of the home to an institution or to relatives.

Typically, a "permanent move" may generally means that neither the borrower nor any other co-borrower has lived in the house continuously for one year or do not intend to live continuously. Bank may obtain such documentary evidence as may be deemed appropriate for the purpose. Settlement of loan along with accumulated interest is to be met by the proceeds received out of sale of residential property or prepayment by borrowers and his next of kin.

The borrower(s) or his/her/their legal heirs estate shall be provided with the first right to settle the loan along with accumulated interest, without sale of property. Bank allows a reasonable time period, say up to 6 months for the house to be sold. The balance surplus (if any), remaining after settlement of the loan with accrued interest and expenses, shall be passed on to the borrower or the estate of the borrower/legal heirs. Borrowers will be required to submit proof of property insurance renewal, tax payment and annual -life certificates in the month of November every year. The life certificate will also include clauses regarding marital status, and permanent residence of the borrowers, in addition to the balance confirmation as on 31st October of that year. Banks also obtain the list of legal heirs at the time of sanction of loan. With a view to avoiding disputes at the time of settlement of loan amount by legal heirs, specific instructions about inheritance of the property and payment of balance amount, if any, of the sale proceeds after settling the bank's dues, will be required to be part of the borrower's will.

Example: Mr. Ram Singh, age 65 years, retired from a private company and his wife Smt. Neeta Rani, age 59 years, reside in their self-occupied and self-owned house at Sector-10 in Chandigarh. He purchased the said house 12 years back in his name for ₹40 lakh. Now present market value of house is Rs100 lakh. He has a fixed deposit of ₹5 lakh in bank.

Mr. Banta Singh who is the son of Mr. Ram Singh is settled in UK and doesn't care about his parents nor does his daughter who is settled in Jaipur.

Smt. Neeta is suffering from a disease and requires ₹5 lakh for treatment. Mr. Ram used his entire life savings for the education of his son. Now he has no money for treatment as well as no arrangement for future earnings. Then someone told them to approach a bank for reverse mortgage loan where rate of interest of loan is @ 12 %. Now friends he has two questions in his mind.

Question No 1: How much amount he would get per month if he uses his Fixed Deposit of ₹5 lakh for his wife's treatment?

Now the loan eligibility is ₹80 Lakh (100*0.80) (80% of market value of property). This loan amount will include interest up to maturity.

Answer 1: Friends now the solution you see is in your hand. See the chart find out column of 12% and find out the number of months for which loan is required (in this case 240 months). You may find out that for per lakh loan he will get Rs101. So, the total amount payable by the bank will be ₹8080 per month.

Loan amount (80) x Per month pay out for one lakh (101).

Question No 2: If he does not use his FD then would he get a lump sum of ₹5 lakh for his wife's treatment and further how much amount he will obtain per month from bank up to maximum time (20 years)?

Answer 2: Yes, he may get lump sum of ₹5 lakhs but in this condition his per month payout will be less. In this condition, loan amount will be divided in two parts. One part will provide ₹5 lakh for current requirement and the other part will supplement the payout.

Monthly Payout Table for 1 Lac Loan

No. of Months	Rate of Interest									
	10.00%	10.75%	11.00%	11.25%	12.00%	12.50%	12.75%	13.00%	13.50%	14.00%
12	7958	7931	7921	7012	7885	7867	7858	7873	7830	7812
24	3781	3753	3744	3735	3707	3689	3680	3671	3653	3635
36	2393	2366	2357	2348	2321	2304	2295	2286	2269	2251
48	1703	1677	1668	1659	1633	1616	1608	1599	1583	1566
60	1291	1266	1258	1249	1224	1208	1200	1192	1176	1160
72	1019	995	987	979	955	939	932	924	909	894
84	827	803	796	788	765	750	743	736	721	707
96	684	662	654	647	625	611	604	507	584	570
108	575	553	546	539	518	505	499	492	470	467
120	483	468	461	454	435	422	416	410	398	386
132	419	399	393	386	368	356	350	344	339	322
144	362	343	337	331	313	302	297	291	281	270
156	315	297	291	285	260	258	253	248	238	223
168	275	258	252	247	231	222	217	212	203	194
180	241	225	220	215	200	191	186	182	173	165
192	213	197	192	188	174	165	161	157	149	141
204	188	173	169	164	151	143	139	135	128	121
216	167	153	148	144	132	124	121	117	110	104
228	148	135	131	127	115	108	105	102	95	89
240	132	119	116	112	101	94	91	88	82	77

❑

39

What Homework should be done before Purchasing a Property from a NRI?

Mr. Aashish Dutt, who is posted in a telecom company called me and asked me could he should purchase a property from an NRI, if yes, then what precaution should be kept in mind. He has a house in his neighborhood which is owned by a NRI lady.

My answer was yes; anyone can purchase property from NRI. But before purchasing property a person has to go through a complex process, because you have to remit money to NRI which is not a part of normal purchasing. Reserve Bank of India and FEMA have provided consent to purchase property from NRI/PIO without any prior approval.

But we have to follow certain steps before purchasing property from NRIs.

First of all, we have to do due diligence of NRI and his property. Because sometimes, the NRI person may pretend that they are resident Indians and can repatriate the sale proceeds their country without paying capital gain taxes in India. It would create a big problem to you. So be assured that person is a non-resident. For the due diligence of NRI we have to visit the place where NRI was living before going abroad. You may ask neighbors about NRI status of person or may check his passport. You may also gather information from his previous employer or business concern with which he was associated.

Due diligence of property should be carried out properly. Ascertain that the NRI is real owner of property and property does not have any dispute associated with it.

If your deal includes a large amount then publish the details of the property in two newspapers one local and other national stating that you are going to purchase the said property and if someone has any objection, they can contact/object within 30 days. It will help you in case any dispute arises in the future regarding ownership of property.

It is not possible for an NRI to come India frequently for purchasing and selling property. So normally a NRI executes a power of attorney, which plays an important role in execution of documents in India.

The NRI does not have to be physically present in India in for the execution of documents in India. The process can be facilitated by one of their representatives (either relative or friend) in India–someone who holds the power of attorney to act on their behalf.

Power of Attorney (POA): It gives an individual the power to act on behalf of another. The scope of the authority granted is as mentioned in the deed. The person who gives the power is referred to as the Principal/Donor/Grantor. The person to whom it is granted is referred to as the Attorney/Donee /Grantee/ Agent.

Normally NRIs issue two type of power of attorney: The first one is the General Power of Attorney and second one is the Special Power of Attorney. A General Power of Attorney is granted when the Agent has to be empowered to conduct many transactions on behalf of the Principal. These could include bank operations, estate operations and other operations while a Special Power of Attorney is granted when the Agent has to conduct only specific transactions.

Execution of Power of Attorney by an NRI may be in two places either in India or Abroad. The power of attorney should be executed on a stamp paper or plain paper (whichever is applicable in the country where the power of attorney is executed). The NRI needs to sign the POA (Power of Attorney) before a consulate officer or a notary in the country where he is residing. The signature on the deed has to then be attested by the consulate officer or notary.

Friends, you should always try to get the POA attested by the Indian consulate, so that it may be considered more authentic. The POA then has to be sent to India, where it should be presented for adjudication within three months.

Adjudication of the POA (Power of Attorney)

Adjudication is the process of registering the POA document in the registrar's office in order for it to be accepted as a registered POA. Once it has been adjudicated, the POA cannot be misused by altering it. After registration, the document will remain with the registration department. A copy of the document can be obtained even after several years after the actual transaction, if anyone wants to verify its authenticity.

Sometimes an NRI can execute a POA and may get it registered in India while they are physically present in the country.

The stamp duty to be paid for the POA registration varies from state to state in India. It is also determined based on the contents of the deed.

Role of Section 195 of Income Tax: The purchaser must know about the section 195 of the income tax act 1961 which is applicable when purchasing a property from NRI. According to this section, tax has to be deducted before making the payment to the seller which is commonly referred to as TDS (tax deducted at source).

Section 195 states that any person responsible for paying a NRI any sum chargeable under the act shall at the time of credit such income to the account of the payee or at the time of payment thereof in cash or by cheque or draft or any other mode, whichever is earlier, deduct income tax thereon at the rates in force.

Friends, remember that section 194-1A which deals with the TDS in real estate transactions is applicable when you purchase a property having sale consideration more than ₹50 lakh from resident Indians. TDS is deducted @ the rate of only 1%; this section is not applicable when you purchase property from NRI.

As per section 195, tax is to be deducted at source as per the rate in force while making payment to NRI. The rate in force is defined under section 2 (37A) 111 Finance Act. Currently, the effective rate in force is 20% on the sale consideration, not on the capital gain derived in the sale transaction. This means that in respect of property owned by NRI, 20% tax is to be deducted regardless of the quantum of sale consideration.

For example, if you purchase a property owned by Mr. D'Souza, who is an NRI, for ₹50 lakh (sale consideration), then the total capital gain is ₹20 lakh. The tax to be deducted is ₹10 lakh (20% of sale consideration) and the balance to be paid to the NRI seller Mr. D'Souza is ₹40 lakh only.

What is the provision on TDS if there is no capital gain in the transaction? Or what is the Provision for getting permission for lower/nil TDS

Mr. D'Souza can also save taxes on the capital gains by reinvesting the sale amount in tax saving bonds or in any other house property in accordance with provisions of the Income Tax Act. If the capital gain amount is reinvested then Mr. D'Souza can reduce his amount of his capital gain. If the entire amount of capital is reinvested then he shall have no tax liability and shall not be liable to pay any taxes. In such a case, Mr. D'Souza also has an option to ask the purchaser to not deduct TDS on the sale consideration. *As per the section 195(2) of income tax act, you can contact your Assessing Officer and can get a certificate for lower or nil deduction of TDS provided as there are no capital gains or the tax payable on capital gain is less than the TDS deducted *Alternatively, u/s 195(3), Mr. D'Souza (payee/NRI) also can approach the Assessing Office and get the certificate. If such a certificate is granted, you (the payer/purchaser of property/person responsible for paying the amount) can make the payment with lower/nil TDS. If such a certificate is not obtained, the payer has to deduct tax, even in case where the property is sold at a loss.

In most of the cases (apart from ones where NRI or buyer gets the permission from the AO) the tax deducted for the NRI would be in excess. NRI needs to file his return of income in India and claim the refund of excess amount.

The Procedure of Deducting TDS

You must deduct TDS on the sales consideration amount before making payment to NRI. Though Mr. D'Souza's capital gain is ₹20 Lakh but the TDS has to be deducted on the entire sales consideration of ₹50 lakh at a rate of 20% which amounts to ₹10

Lakh. A PAN card is mandatory for both parties in case of such transactions. It is the responsibility of the purchaser to deposit the taxes so deducted (by using challan for payment of TDS) with the government (through banks authorized to collect direct taxes) within seven days from the end of the month in which such a tax has been deducted.

Once the TDS has been paid, you should file the TDS returns electronically, within the due dates as applicable by providing all the details of Mr. D'Souza which would include his address, PAN etc. After filing the TDS returns electronically, you may issue the TDS certificate in Form 16A to Mr. D'Souza, within 15 days from the due date of furnishing TDS returns. Friends, remember, if you fail to deduct or fail to pay the amount deducted by you then you will be treated as Assessee in Default as per section 201 of the Income Tax Act, 1961 and will be liable for payment of interest, penalties and prosecution.

Claiming of Refund of Excess TDS paid

It is very clear that if TDS has been deducted on the sales consideration, excess taxes have been paid to the income tax department. Mr. D'Souza is liable to claim refund of the excess taxes, deducted by you, from the department by mentioning the details of the sale and capital gain in his Income Tax Return for the Assessment Year. He has to file his return within the due date to claim the refund of the excess taxes paid. Upon successful processing of the return, if all details are mentioned correctly, the refund amount would be paid to Mr. D'Souza by the income tax department.

Repatriation of Funds

NRI's mostly want to reinvest the sale proceed received in a new property outside India or they simply want to take their funds along with them to a foreign bank account or their NRE account in India. If Mr. D'Souza wants to transfer the funds received by sale from his NRO account to his NRE or Foreign Bank account, he is required to submit a certificate which is Form 15CB signed by a Chartered Accountant, to the bank certifying that the right amount of tax has been deducted or the reason for non-deduction of TDS. He is also required to file Form 15CA online with the details of the Form 15CB certificate. Upon submission of the form Mr. D'Souza can freely repatriate his funds outside India.

Finally, if you are buying a property from NRI and the whole procedure is too cumbersome for you to handle then you may take help of a Charted Accountant.

❑

40

What is Estate Planning?

When a person has done proper real estate planning, his next step is to do proper estate planning. Estate Planning is a process of arranging and planning a person's succession and financial affairs. An Estate Plan which incorporates a person's wishes about his estate could be regarding as Estate Management, Estate Preservation and Estate Legacy during and post life. It means it will enhance and maintain your and your family's financial security by accumulation, conservation and distribution of an Estate.

The ultimate goal of estate planning is to fulfill the estate owner's wishes as closely as possible by ensuring that the estate of the individual passes to the estate owner's intended beneficiaries, often including efficient tax and succession planning and avoiding or minimizing court proceedings in succession matters and obtaining probates.

Estate Duty was introduced in India in 1953 and was abolished in 1985. Today we have no estate tax or estate duty unlike many advanced countries. Also, if Estate Duty is reinstated in India today or in the near future, Estate Planning may turn out to be the best tool to minimize the Estate Duty. Estate planning by Trust Structures was primarily done to minimize Estate Duty/ Tax which is imposed on all property transferred at death.

Some people may see no need for estate planning until they reach a certain age, or they might believe that only Estate planning provides you financial security during the retirement years and to facilitate the intended and orderly disposition of property at death. We cannot predicate our time of death. Estate planning should begin as soon as you have property or dependents. Estates are essentially property.

An individual's estate is made up of all the property he or she owns and controls till the moment of death. Estate planning involves planning for disposition of the property. Every estate is planned in a sense. Now a question may arise in your mind that who should draft and design your estate plan. The chapters in this book will help you in this process. You can also take help from a certified financial planner or a lawyer.

With Estate Planning, a person can preserve and protect his or her estate and have his or her wishes carried out after death. Without purposeful planning, a lifetime of work and dreams could be squandered.

Estate planning is not just for the wealthy. It is for anyone who owns property and has preferences as to whom, how, and when that property is transferred at his or her death. A rich person can reap great benefits from the tax aspects of estate planning. However, individuals with the smallest estates are also likely to benefit by attaining financial security for their families through financial and estate planning.

Proper Estate Planning answers the following questions.

- What will happen if I become ill?
- Who will make decisions about the type of care I receive if I become physically disabled or mentally incompetent?

- How do I want my property distributed?
- What happens if I just do nothing?
- Will there be huge bills to pay?
- Where will the money to pay these bills come from?
- Are there ways to reduce estate settlement costs?
- Are there sufficient assets to support a surviving spouse?
- Are there ways to ease the financial burdens faced by my children?
- Is it possible to help grandchildren for education?
- How can I best make gifts to the charitable organizations I support?

What is the Purpose and Need of Estate Planning?

Why is estate planning so important? Because it allows you to accomplish a number of crucial objectives like; harmonious and planned succession and disposition of the estate which helps ensure that your money and other assets go to the people you choose. If you become unable to work or survive, then to take care of unforeseen eventualities by providing support to your minor children.

The basic purpose is to provide support to a widow who has no job and has two or more children. If her husband had a sound estate plan she will not suffer. There will be proper arrangement for her children after the death of her husband. For younger couples, there is a greater chance that both spouses will have begun to establish some financial security. Each partner may have retirement benefits from his or her own employment. Still, when one partner dies, there will usually be a reduction in income for the survivor. In the early stages of employment, the amount of pension is generally less. So again, estate planning is necessary to compensate for the shortfall.

In most estate planning, providing for children is the second major concern after providing for the surviving spouse. For small estates, the normal course of action is that all property should pass on to the surviving spouse with distribution to children at the second death. For larger estates planning for the ultimate distribution to children often begins while both the husband and wife are still living, since nowadays divorce and remarriage are becoming common in Indian families.

It is not uncommon to find families with children from different marriages. This can create problem for a person who has children from more than one wife. Will all children be treated equally? If everything passes to the second spouse, will he or she distribute the assets to all the children or only to his or her natural children? Couples faced with these kinds of situation must do estate planning. A common solution is to use trusts to provide for the surviving spouse while leaving the corpus (assets) in trust for the named beneficiaries of the deceased.

Implementation of an estate plan requires an individual to acknowledge the reality of his or her mortality. Very few people can deal comfortably with this. There are many sophisticated and successful professionals who are quite at ease in the high-pressure environment of finance and international business but are so reluctant to acknowledge the inevitability of death that they never implement a cohesive estate plan.

Ultimately, members of the estate owner's family are the ones who suffer when this happens. Their standard of living is impaired at the decedent's death, or they are forced to impose some semblance of order on an estate that is in disarray. Hence estate planning is the foremost judicious step in securing your family's future and fulfilling your desires during your life and after you depart from the world.

❑

41

Role of Insurance in Estate Planning

The role of life insurance in your estate plan is quite important. It can help financially by offering your family long term replacement of the lost income and benefits and by providing liquidity for immediate costs such as medical bills and funeral expenses. It can also provide the peace of mind, knowing that if something happened to you, your family wouldn't be left financially insecure. Life insurance is present in almost every estate plan and serves as a source of support, education-expense coverage and liquidity to pay death taxes, pay expenses, fund business buy-sell agreements and sometimes to fund retirement plans.

Proceeds from life insurance that are received by the beneficiaries upon the death of the Insured are generally incomes tax-free.

When a person purchases a property with loan, he takes a liability to repay it timely. But some unforeseen circumstances like disability, death and natural calamities may cause problems. So every person who takes a loan, also must think about two types of insurance. Friends, what happens if a person who takes a loan without any insurance suddenly dies? If his wife is a housewife, she has only one option which is to sell the property and repay the entire loan. Now family has to face two losses, one is earning member, second is the shelter.

Two types of insurance are compulsory for a prudent home loan customer.

1. **Borrower Own Life Insurance Equal to Home Loan Amount:** Normally the head of family is the main earning member of the family. He takes a home loan for his dream house. He pays an EMI which is the most part of his salary or business income. Untimely death causes problems in the payment of EMI. Banks ask his legal heir to pay the entire outstanding loan. When the family is unable to pay outstanding of the loan then bank sells his property which causes further grief to the already bereaved family members. If a person has home loan cover, then the bank receives outstanding money from insurer and account is closed and the family gets rid of the loan and gets their house back from the lender.

   These are normally of two types:

   (i) Traditional Term Plan (ii) Tailor made- Decreasing Term Assurance Plan.

   (i) ***Traditional Term Plan:*** This is a pure insurance plan which has low premium without return. On death, an assured full sum assured is returned to beneficiaries. Suppose a person requires a term plan of ₹30 lakh for his life cover and now he takes a home loan of ₹20 lakh. He should require minimum cover of ₹50 lakh. When untimely death of this person occurs, the insurance amount received will support his family. His family gets ₹50 lakh, family members repay the ₹20 lakh against their home loan and rest amount can be used for their livelihood. The main benefit of this type of cover is that person always gets full amount of cover equal to insurance obtained.

(ii) ***Tailor made:*** Decreasing Term Assurance Plan - It is a decreasing term insurance plan. The plan provides high sum assured at a lower one time premium but does not provide any maturity benefits to the customer. People in the age group of 18 - 65 years can be covered under this plan. Coverage ceases with the expiry of the term of the loan.

At any point of time from the start of cover, surrender value is available subject to loan being fully repaid before the end of the term. Nomination is compulsory under this plan. It also provides for the income tax benefits u/s 80C. In this policy a person who takes insurance is called Group Member and the bank which gives the home loan is called as Master Policy Holder.

Salient Features

❖ Life cover for the entire period of the loan equivalent to the outstanding loan amount

❖ In the event of death, the Insurance Company pays the balance loan (as per original EMI Schedule) directly to the bank, thus providing complete freedom to the family. However, the overdue amount, if any, is not covered.

❖ Insurance premium paid is eligible for tax rebate under section 80C of Income Tax act with an overall ceiling of ₹1,50,000/-

❖ The death claim is tax free in the hands of the nominee / assignee under Section 10 (10) D of Income Tax Act.

❖ Protects the borrower against death due to any reason.

- Insurance cover up to age 70 of the borrower, or the last date of repayment, whichever is earlier? Normally loans are also sanctioned up to age of 70 years.
- Single premium for the entire duration of the loan. Bank may provide additional loan to cover the premium amount.
- Hassle-free joining process.
- Premium payable determined based on Loan Amount, Term sof repayment and age of the borrower.

Exclusion

- Will not cover if death occurs within first 45 days from the commencement of insurance cover.
- Death due to suicide during the first 12 months from the commencement of insurance.

Which Plan is the Best? Use a term plan to cover your home loan liability. You will be better off opting for a term plan rather than a onetime tailor-made decreasing term plan (also known as home loan protection plan) for a number of reasons. One, term plans are cheaper than tailor- made ones decreasing term assurance plan. Two, it is easier to compare the term plans offered by different insurers as premium, riders and sum insured options are the standard factors for evaluation. On the other hand, a bank offers a single option for tailor made decreasing term assurance plan. The customer doesn't get the benefit of comparing prices and can end up paying a much higher premium than the best plan available in the market.

Another disadvantage of tailor-made decreasing term assurance plan is that the payment is often through a single premium. If you prepay the loan before the full tenure say, a 15-year loan within 10 years you will lose the premium paid for the remaining term as that money is not refunded or if otherwise refunded this will be very less.

Finally, in case you transfer the home loan from one bank to another for the lower interest charged by the latter, there could be hassles in porting the home loan protection plan. Since the term cover is separate from the home loan, you can keep it or modify it according to your needs.

2. **House Insurance:** Normally in all banks, house/property insurance is compulsory if a person takes home loan from bank. Insurance safeguards against unforeseen natural and man-made calamities such as fire, earthquake, avalanche and terrorist strike etc.

Simple Cover (Fire and Allied Perils Policy)

This policy covers the house structure with its material from loss due to fire, cyclone, earth quake, strike, terrorist strike, etc. It is based on reinstatement value of house instead of market value. (Reinstatement value is the cost to rebuilt/repair a house in the same condition as before it was.) Suppose there is a house in good condition and it is damaged due to a natural or manmade calamity. Now it requires money to repair or rebuilt in the same position as before house was. Though insurance company pays the required money to rebuilt or repair it but it does not pay the amount for the entire construction. When a house is damaged due to above mentioned perils, then only insurance may help you. Although a house is the most valuable asset for any individual and home insurance is very cheap in India, yet, very few people insure their home. The vital covers your house needs will cost you less than ₹2000 a year. Keep in mind that you don't need to insure the house for the value of the property but only for the reinstatement value (cost of reconstructing it.) The costs can vary from ₹1,000 per sq ft for a basic no-frills structure to ₹2,500 per sq ft for a premium construction. You also need to insure the contents of the house against damage.

Fire insurance is designed to provide for financial loss property due to fire and a few other related hazards. Fire insurance is governed by a Tariff under the Tariff Advisory committee (TAC). Examples of contents that can be covered under the Fire insurance policy are:

1 **Building:** Contents of buildings (Machinery, equipment, accessories), goods, raw materials, semi-finished/finished goods, packing materials etc. stored in factories and godowns, electrical installations of a building, goods in the open, dwellings and contents of dwellings, furniture, fixture and fittings, pipelines located inside and outside buildings, dwellings and compounds.

2 Explosion/Implosion, Aircraft damage, Lightning, Storm, cyclone, typhoons, tempest hurricane, tornado, flood and inundation, Subsidence and Landslide including rock slides, Riot, Bush Fire, Impact by any rail/road vehicle or animal by direct contact, strike, malicious and terrorism damage.

House Holder Policy

The covers against burglary and breakage are costlier but important nevertheless. You can further enhance the coverage by adding more sections if you perceive a certain risk and if your pocket allows.

A standard fire and allied perils policy covers damage due to fire, lightning, storm, flood, landslide, earthquake, shock, explosion, storm, tempest, hurricane, subsidence vehicle impact, rioting, arson and bursting of pipes and tanks. It is possible to buy this as a standalone cover, but most insurance companies encourage buyers to go for a comprehensive plan that covers a wide range of risks.

Some people think they don't need home insurance if they live in a rented house. While this is true, they still need insurance against any damage to the contents (by any natural or man-made disaster) and against burglary. These basic covers don't cost too much. When you have worked hard to be able to own a home, shouldn't you go the extra step to make sure that both the house and the valuables within it are protected from misfortune?

Precaution while taking insurance

1. If you purchase a property using a home loan then you must always give preference to the insurance company with whom your banker has a tie-up. The benefit of this is that when there is a loss bank may directly demand claim from insurance company.
2. Premium term should be equal to the loan tenure. If we select single premium, then we get discount.
3. Always remember that in case of house insurance land value should not be included in cost of house because land cannot be destroyed.
4. Always insure your valuable assets (AC, LED) on replacement value not on the depreciated value.
5. If your family purchases new jewelry, or any electronic item then inform the insurance company and always keep these items in bank locker after using them on occasions.

❑

42

Will

A Will is a legal declaration of a person's intention with respect to his property, which he desires to be carried into effect after his death. Thus, a Will operates only after the death of the person. We know that writing a Will has been a traditional way of passing on all what a person has earned and what he has inherited from his ancestors to his future generations.

Anyone and everyone who wants his assets to go to his heirs without any glitch should write a Will. It's a myth that only the super-rich need to write Wills. The fact is that anyone and everyone should write a Will so that his heirs do not face difficulties in accessing what is rightfully theirs. Any adult who wants to distribute his assets can write a Will. The assets can be anything property, gold, financial investments, art and artifacts, even hard cash lying at home. Contrary to perception, it is not necessary to write it on a stamp paper or even get it registered. You can write a Will on plain paper and it will be as legally valid as one prepared by a lawyer. All it should do is identify you as the testator (or the person who is making the Will), list out your assets and specify how these are to be distributed among the beneficiaries. Whether you type it out or write it down, so long as the Will is signed by you and attested by two witnesses, it is a legal document for all practical purposes.

For most people, Will making can be a do-it-yourself exercise. The only requirement is that the Will should be legible. However, if your assets and ownership are a little complicated, you may need the help of a legal professional to draft the Will. He would ensure that there are no loopholes or ambiguity in the language that may lead to disputes in future. More importantly, he would make sure that the distribution is within the ambit of the law.

If a person is old and frail, he should avoid writing it himself and get it typed to avoid disputes among his heirs. A Will cannot override the natural succession of ancestral wealth. In other words, a person cannot Will away inherited property to the exclusion of the legal heirs of that property. Suppose a Hindu man inherits ₹50 lakh from his father. If he has four legal heirs, then he has only 20% share in that ₹50 lakh. The balance belongs to the four legal heirs. He can Will his own share (Rs 10 lakh) as he pleases but cannot distribute the balance ₹40 lakh to somebody other than the four heirs. It is important for you to make a Will regardless of your financial status.

Why it is Important to Make a Will?

- If you die without a Will, there are certain rules which dictate how the money, property or possessions should be allocated. This may not be the way that you would have wished your money and possessions to be distributed.
- Unmarried partners and partners who have not registered a civil partnership cannot inherit from each other unless there is a Will, so the death of one partner may create serious financial problems for the remaining partner.

- If you have children, you will need to make a Will so that arrangements for the children can be made if either one or both parents die.
- It may be possible to reduce the amount of tax payable on the inheritance if advice is taken in advance and a Will is made.
- If your circumstances have changed, it is important that you make a Will to ensure that your money and possessions are distributed according to your wishes. For example, if you have separated and your ex-partner now lives with someone else, you may want to change your Will. If you are married or enter into a registered civil partnership, this Will make any previous Will you have made invalid.

Characteristics of a Will

A Will is a legal declaration of the intention of a testator with respect to his property, which he desires to be carried into effect after his death. It includes codicil and every writing making a voluntary posthumous disposition of property. It is testamentary instrument by which a person makes disposition of his property to take effect after his death, and which, in its own nature. It is revocable during his life. Thus, a Will can be changed by the executants as and when he so likes. It is a secret and confidential document which the executants is never ordered to produce.

There are two essential characteristics of a Will-

1. It must be intended to come into effect after the death of the testator.
2. It must be revocable by the testator at any time.

Although Wills are usually made for disposing property, they can also be made for appointing executors, for creating trusts and for appointing testamentary guardians of minor children.

You should keep in mind one important thing that contents of the Will must indicate that it is intended to come into effect only after death of testator and that it is revocable at any time prior to his death and a document cannot be treated as a Will by a mere heading. Sec 63 of the Indian Succession Act, 1925 provides that a Will is liable to be revoked or altered by its maker at any time when he is competent to dispose of his property by Will.

When a person dies without making a Will, he is said to have died intestate. His property is then inherited by his legal heirs in accordance with the law of inheritance applicable to him. It must be noted here that legal heirs generally include close family members such as one's spouse, children, parents etc. However, most of the people would like to dispose of their property according to their own wishes. Thus, there arises the need for making one's Will.

Hindu Law of Succession

As per Hindu Law of Succession, relations are divided into two classes.

Class 1 and Class 2 .Class 1 legal heirs have the first right on the property and only if there is no one left into Class 1, then Class 2 legal heirs are considered. The following table lists relation that come under Class 1 & 2. Each of them has equal right in the wealth.

Class 1 (First priority)	Class 2 (are considered only if Class 1 is not present)
1. Mother	1. Father
2. Widow (Wife of the deceased)	2. Brother/Sister
3. Son/Daughter	3. Parents of dead parents
4. Widow of dead son	4. Siblings of dead parents
5. Grandchildren	5. Children of siblings

6. Widow of grandson	6. Widow of brother
7. Children of grandson	7. Great grandchildren of dead daughter
	8. Children of dead daughter of dead son

One share for each - Each category gets one share each and under each category if there are more than 1 person, they will divide the share between them equally. For example if the person C whose wealth is to be divided had 2 children A and B, who are both dead, but A had 1 child and B had 2 children. Then for C, A and B are the main legal heirs, who are entitled for equal share (50% each), but now their children will get it. So A's child will get 50% share , but B's children will get 25 % share each, so for B, the 50% part will be divided equally into his 2 children.

So your next action is very clear. Just look at your family and identify who will be your legal heirs in case a will is missing. They will get a share in your wealth if you do not write a will. Even if the division looks perfect, that's not an excuse to skip writing the Will. So just get hold of a good lawyer in your city (or online) and get it prepared and yes, don't forget to register the will.

Contents of a Will

To save time and reduce costs when going to a solicitor, you should keep in mind all the major points which you want to include in your will. You should consider such things as:

- How much movable and immovable property you have, for example, savings, occupational and personal pensions, mutual fund investments, shares, property, insurance policies, bank and building society accounts.

- Who you want to benefit from your Will? You should make a list of all the people to whom you wish to leave money or possessions. These people are known as beneficiaries. You also need to consider whether you wish to leave any money to charity.
- Who should look after any children under 18?
- Who is going to sort out the estate and carry out your wishes as set out in the Will? These people are known as the executors.

Apart from It There Are Certain Distinct Advantages Of Making A Will

- When a person dies without having made a Will, there is often confusion amongst the family members and relatives whether the deceased did make any Will prior to his death or not. However, if a Will is available, the only question that needs to be ascertained is whether it is the last Will of the testator.
- A Will is absolutely a personal document. Basically, it is an expression of the relationship with the members of family or relatives, etc. The views, opinions and feelings are indicated in this document. A Will allows the distribution of property in a personalized manner rather than letting the impersonal rules of inheritance take effect.
- Many disputes can be resolved at the very outset if there is a clear disposition of one's property in a Will.
- By means of a Will, one can appoint in writing, a testamentary guardian for his infant children. A testamentary guardian is a person, who is appointed in a testament or a Will. You should remember that in the event of the death of a parent the law would ordinarily uphold the right of surviving natural parent to be the guardian of the child. However, if there is

no surviving parent, the law attaches great importance to the Will of a parent in deciding who to appoint as a guardian. This is a matter of great importance with regard to the future of the children and therefore, this issue must be discussed in detail with the proposed guardian before appointing him a testamentary guardian.

- A Will provides more room than the laws of inheritance, which sometimes do not cater to the special needs and requirements of the members of a family. Suppose a person has two sons. One is healthy and in service but the other is handicapped due to polio. The laws of inheritance would treat both these children on an equal footing. But by means of a Will, a father has somewhat greater provision for a handicapped son, a widowed daughter, etc. Not only that but by means of a Will, one can make some provision for a faithful servant, a nurse, a friend in need of money, and so on. All such people could never receive any benefit whatsoever through the laws of inheritance in the absence of a Will.
- In the absence of a Will even the most unwanted son, who has left the house for disobedience, fraud violence, etc. may turn up to claim his share of estate from his father's property. Similarly, an adulterous wife might demand her share as per inheritance laws.

Disadvantages of Making a Will.

There are however, some disadvantages also in making a Will and they are mostly psychological. In many cases it has been observed that people lose all their interests in life and the same such before the time they would have lived.

If there is no Will, the property would be dealt with as per the laws of inheritance. For Hindus, Buddhists, Jains and Sikhs the laws of inheritance have been codified in the Hindu Succession Act, 1956. For Christians, the Indian Succession Act, 1925 will be applicable. Muslims have their own law. Similarly, Parsis have a different law of inheritance.

Requirements for a Valid Will

- It should be made by a major person who is 18 years old or over. A minor being of immature understanding cannot be said to be of sound mind and as such incapable of making a Will.
- A married woman may dispose any property by Will which she could alienate by her own act during her life.
- A person of a sound mind can make a Will. This means the person must be fully aware of the nature of the document being written or signed and aware of the property and the identity of the people who may inherit.
- A Will should be made voluntarily and without pressure from any other person.
- Persons who are deaf or dumb or blind can make a Will provided they are able to know what they do by it.
- A person who is ordinarily insane may make a Will during an interval in which he is of sound mind.

Some Common Mistakes in making A Will Are

- Not being aware of the formal requirements needed to make a Will legally valid.
- Failing to take account of all the money and property available.
- Failing to take account of the possibility that a beneficiary may die before the person making the Will.
- Changing the Will. If these alterations are not signed and witnessed, they are invalid.
- Being unaware of the effect of marriage, a registered civil partnership, divorce or dissolution of a civil partnership or a Will.

- Being unaware of the rules which exist to enable dependents to claim from the estate if they believe they are not adequately provided for. These rules mean that the provisions in the Will could be overturned.
- When it is particularly advisable to use a Solicitor.

How to Draft a Will?

Before drafting a Will sit in a peaceful and separate room or place. Keep in mind all the contents of the Will. First of all take a pencil and plain white paper and make a list of your all assets of two types movable and immovable. Immovable assets include plot, house, flat, farmhouse, industrial land, commercial land, factory, etc. While all others assets are classified as movable assets. Ensure that all items are included.

Now prepare the list of all near and dear and finalize those relatives or non-relatives to whom you want to bequeath assets. These persons are called beneficiaries. Friends, always write full name which are mentioned in documents of person (in PAN Card, Passport or 10th Mark Sheet) with father's name of beneficiaries so that time of execution or assets distribution of Will there would be no confusion of name if family is joint and large.

The third step is to write down different family liabilities, commitments to other persons or any obligation to someone. In some families there may be unmarried daughter or a divorced daughter whose marriage needs to be solemnized and funds are required in near future so make provision in Will. There may be a nephew or niece who is an orphan and living with testator family or in testator family there may be a physically or mentally handicapped, for his/her smooth livelihood testator has to make some provisions in Will. As a testator, you have to consider all these obligations or liabilities and write down in paper so that you would be sure to fulfill all commitment and liabilities.

If you have any home loan or any other loan then make provision and fix liability of particular member (to whom you want to bequeath the asset) to repay the loan.

The fourth step is to make a list of assets with beneficiary's name. Ensure that no item and no beneficiaries should to be left from the list. Now the rough format of your Will is ready for further steps.

Who should Draft Your Will either you or Your Lawyer?

This is also an important step for you as a testator (a person who is going to write a Will) that who should draft your Will. For this purpose, you could either contact a lawyer or write your Will yourself. There is no particular format or a particular language for writing a Will by law, so it's easy to write your own Will if you wish to. Any professional lawyer, your financial planner or any literate person can draft a Will but he must keep your interest and sentiments in mind. Draft Wills are found in many legal books or on internet.

As per law, Wills made by Hindus, Jains, Buddhists and Sikhs are required to be in writing, signed by the testator or any person in his presence by his direction, and attested by at least two witnesses. You must note that this requirement does not apply for Muslims.

The language used in the Will should be as simple as possible and should be free from technical words. It should be easily intelligible to a layman.

Executors

As the Will requires mentioning of an executor for executing the Will, the Executor's role starts after death of testator. Executors are the people who will be responsible for carrying out our wishes and for sorting out the estate. They will have to collect together all the assets of the estate, deal with all the paperwork and pay all the debts, taxes, and funeral and administration costs out of money in the estate. They will need to pay out the gifts and transfer any property to beneficiaries.

A single person (male or female) or joint executors can be nominated as an executor of the Will. Normally relatives or friends or solicitors or accountants and banks are nominated as executors. When a lady is appointed as an executor, she is known as an executrix of the Will.

The executor has the powers, rights and duties to distribute the assets of the testator according to the specific direction contained in the Will. Since the executor assignment involves a great deal of work and responsibility, so you should select an honest person with considerable care who is concerned about the welfare of the testator's family. But keep in mind, that the person should be agree to take on the responsibility. Executor's age should be lesser than age of testator.

You are advised to appoint more than one executor; in case one of them may die. So it is common practice to appoint two, but up to four executors. There is no problem even in appointing one of the beneficiaries of your Will as the executor. If an executor dies, any other surviving executor(s) can deal with the estate. If there are no surviving executors, legal advice should be sought.

Witnesses

Before you start drafting a will, you should think about the selection of witnesses. A Will has to be attested by at least two witnesses, in the presence of the person making the Will, after it has been signed a witness or the married partner of witness who cannot derive any benefit from the Will. Without a witness signature, a Will is void. A witness may be any person either male or female but the witness should neither be beneficiaries nor interested in the property. You should select at least two witnesses in a Will. Their selection criteria are same as that of the executor. It means they should be honest to you and ready to sign your Will. They should be younger than the testator. They should also be available at the time of execution or registration of the Will.

Solicitor

There is no need for a will to be drawn up or witnessed by a solicitor. If you wish to make a Will yourself; you can do so. However, you should only consider doing this if the Will is going to be straightforward.

It is generally advisable to use a solicitor or to have a solicitor check a Will you have drawn up to make sure it Will has the effect you want. This is because it is easy to make mistakes and, if there are errors in the Will, this can cause problems after your death. Sorting out misunderstandings and disputes may result in considerable legal costs, which may reduce the amount of money available in the estate.

It Is Particularly Advisable to Use A Solicitor In The Following Circumstances.

- There is a business involved.
- You share a property with someone who is not your husband, wife or civil partner.
- There are several family members who may make a claim on the Will, for example, a second wife or children from a first marriage.
- You are not an Indian citizen.
- You wish to make provision for an invalid dependent.
- Your permanent home is not in India.
- You are resident here but there is overseas property involved.

Prepare Separate Wills for Separate Property for Separate Individuals

If you have more than one property and legal heirs, then you should think about some important points.

Dr. K Y Manohar is retired physician and living in Mumbai. Now he is 68 years old and thinks that it is right time to draft a will. He has two sons and one daughter. All are married. While in service, he purchased three different properties at different locations in India. These include his bungalow in which he is currently living with his wife Mrs. Kamla and youngest son. He also has a house in Delhi and a flat in Jaipur.

His eldest son Mr. Rajeev is a GM in a multinational company and the son is running chain of restaurants. In his Will, Dr. Manohar mentioned each of his children's names and bequeathed each a property. He ensured that his daughter also got one of his properties. He then registered the Will.

In September 2014 when I visited him, he showed me the Will and asked my opinion.

Now it was not a challenge for a Certified Financial Planner to explain him that he was right or wrong.

Before discussing the answer to this question, I would like to mention a critical point, since I am associated with housing loan also.

Some time ago, a customer showed me a photocopy of a chain of documents which included a Will and pertaining to a particular property they wanted to purchase. During the discussion, they said that they could only produce a certified copy of the Will and Probate since the Will was made for the entire family. Hence, the seller was not able to provide the original Will. Hence, this led to a situation where it was upon the discretion of the loan manager to approve the home loan for the customer.

To avoid a similar situation, I asked Dr. Manohar to prepare separate Wills for his children for each of his properties.

It means a single property single Will with single legal heir. I suggested him to prepare three separate and independent Wills for separate property for separate individuals.

Main advantages of independent and separate Will in relation to each property is that the person who is going to inherit the property can inherit such property a without any difference from any other family member. You know that Dr. Manohar had executed only one combined Will for properties. Whenever Mr. Manohar dies, issues mainly related to subsequent sale of properties will arise. The main reason of these problems would be that there would be just one document (his Will) to dictate the distribution of his assets to different family members. At a later date when any of these family members decide to sell a portion of the property or the entire property, they will face issues since there is only one document through which all members became owners of different properties inherited by them and they will not be able to provide the original Will to the purchaser which may lead to doubts on the purchaser's part.

I suggested that he should draft the first Will in name of Mr. Rajeev to bequeath his residential house situated at Delhi. Second Will was for his daughter who was settled in Jaipur with her husband in which Dr. Manohar mentioned the flat situated in Jaipur. Dr. Manohar told me that his purpose for purchasing property in Jaipur was basically for his daughter. I asked him to write a sentence in each Will that he has other Wills for his other properties.

His youngest son Mr. Anil and his family were living with Dr. Manohar and his wife. Now the third Will was to be drafted which was related to his current residential property in Mumbai. I told him some facts which were related to his wife's safety and security after his death. His wife was five years younger than Dr.

Manohar. When a person dies, his son or daughter looks after his wife in old age. But all people are not equal. Some sons or daughters after getting property through Will and probate force their mother to go old age home or provide a little space for living like servant quarter or garage portion for remaining life. This is a horrible situation for any elderly person and friends this situation may happen with anyone.

To avoid this situation, I told Dr. Manohar some points to write in the Will which was to be executed for his youngest son. The points which was to be written clearly in Will was that his wife (Mrs. Kamla) would occupy exactly the same space/area/ portion in his residential house which was occupied by her prior to his (Dr. Manohar) death, including the drawing room/guest room, bedroom, the bathrooms and toilets, the prayer room as well as the garden of the house. My dear Friends, mentioning this point in Will is necessary for everyone so that wife can enjoy the right to stay or use her husband's house after his death of her husband or any other relative, in tune with the Will of that person.

The fourth and final Will was related to all movable assets like bank balance, shares, mutual fund, bank FD, jewelry, etc.

Now the whole exercise was completed. So, everyone should draft his Will in this manner. The whole process should be recorded on video and the Will should be registered in the office of the Sub- Registrar.

You can either keep a copy of the will at home or with a solicitor or at a bank.

Modifying or Revoking of a Will

A Will is liable to be revoked or altered by its maker at any time when he is competent to dispose of his property by Will. If you wish to make major changes to a Will; it is advisable to make a new one. The new Will should begin with a clause stating that it revokes all previous Wills and codicils. The old Will should be destroyed. Revoking a Will means that the Will is no longer legally valid.

Codicils

A codicil is a supplement to a Will which makes some alterations but leaves the rest of it intact. This might be done, for example, to increase a cash legacy, change an executor or guardian named in a Will, or to add beneficiaries.

There is no limit on how many codicils can be added to a will, but they are only suitable for very straightforward changes. If a complicated change is involved, it is usually advisable to make a new Will. A codicil must be signed by the person who made the Will and be witnessed in the same way. However, the witnesses do not have to be the same as for the original Will.

Probate

A probate is a copy of a Will certified by a court of competent jurisdiction. It proves that it is the last and final Will of the deceased penned on a particular date. A probate is granted with the court seal and has a copy of the Will attached to it. An administrator or executor appointed under the Will may not be able to administer its provisions without a probate. It may also be necessary when the deceased leaves behind securities with various nominees and there is a dispute on their division. The nominee can only hold the assets in trust till these are divided as indicated in the Will after a probate has been obtained. In the absence of a Will or nomination, succession laws come into play.

- **Application:** The application for a probate has to be made to the competent court (a pecuniary jurisdiction may require a higher court to issue a probate for high-value immovable assets) through a lawyer.

- **Documents:** The court usually asks the petitioner to establish the proof of death of testator, proof that the Will has been validly executed by the testator, and that it is the last Will and testament of the deceased.
- **Notification:** After receiving the petition or application for probate, the court issues a notice to the next of kin of the deceased to file objections, if any, to the granting of probate. It also directs the publication of a citation in a newspaper to notify the general public.
- **Fees:** The court may impose a percentage of assets as a fee to issue a probate. In Maharashtra, for example, a court fee of ₹25 is payable for assets less than ₹50,000; 4% for assets between ₹50,000-2 lakh, and 7.5% for assets over ₹2 lakh. There is a ceiling of ₹75000. Point to be noted that under the India Succession Act, a probate can be granted only to the executor appointed under a Will.

If the executor is not available to administer the estate, an application must be made for appointing the same by the court before applying for probate. A probate is a must when the Will is for immovable assets in Mumbai, Kolkata or Chennai. The probate court is only concerned with the question as to whether the document put forward as the last Will of the deceased person was duly executed and attested. The court is also to see whether at the time of the execution of that document whether the testator had sound disposing mind. The probate court is not to embark on the question relating to disputed questions of title and possession.

Unprivileged Wills: Wills executed according to the provisions of Sec 63 of the Indian Succession Act are called Unprivileged Wills.

Privileged Wills: Wills executed under Sec 66 of the Act, by a soldier employed in an expedition or engaged in actual warfare, or by an airman so employed or engaged, or by a mariner being at sea, are called Privileged Wills, it is provided in the Act that such a Will may be written wholly by the testator with his own hands and, in such a case, it need not be signed or attested; or it may be written wholly or in part by another person, in which case, it may be signed by the testator but need not be attested.

Joint Wills: From last decades, may women are also in jobs, so a couple normally purchase a property with joint name for taking home loan as well as tax benefit. For such types of property, which are in joint name, a joint Will is executed. A joint Will is a testamentary instrument whereby two or more persons agree to make a conjoint Will. Where a Will is joint and is intended to take effect after the death of both, it will not be enforceable during the life-time of either. Joint Wills are revocable anytime by either of the testators during their joint lives, or after the death of one, by the survivor.

❑

43

e-Will (Latest Best Option)

These days, it is possible to make Wills on the internet. So now, you can also make a Will online. Recently two e-Will writing services have been launched. One of them is provided by a joint venture of NSDL e-Governance Infrastructure with Mumbai-based Warmond Trustees and Executors. The product launched by this venture is Ezee Will and is available as www.ezeewill.com on NSDL. And second other through a joint venture of HDFC Securities Ltd with Legal Jini. These two ventures will help to complete the last leg of one's financial planning—succession planning-online. The e-will service is an addition to the bouquet of online services that the firm offers. The basic purpose of these services is to simplify the Will writing process.

Procedure for drafting an e-will

Before you start drafting an e-Will, you should complete an exercise which includes a list of items to be included, list of people with father's name to whom you want to bequeath assets as well as some important consideration like unmarried daughter's marriage expanses, provision for a family member who is handicapped. After doing this little exercise you may start drafting the e-Will. To draft an e-Will, the customer needs to register and create a login ID then pay the fee online using debit card/credit card or net banking facility. Third step is related to furnish general detail like your gender, age, occupation, religion, status (Indian or NRI), etc.

Now come to fourth stage where you have to fill all family members' details, your own assets and how you want to bequeath and distribute your assets to your near and dear ones. In every step you should save the information filled by you so that the data can be saved on service provider's website and you can fill entire details at your convenience. Once the data has been filled in, click on submit and generate a will on the prescribed format. Now, this information will be forwarded by the website to its iegal experts, who will draft the Will, which is then delivered to you via an email or at your doorstep via speed post. You may draft the Will from anywhere you like. However, there is a time frame involved. For instance, HDFC Securities gives you 60 days from the date of payment to fill in all the details.

Will writing requirements and laws may differ from case to case and from community to community. The e-Will service providers take into account the succession act that applies to a customer's religion and community. In fact, they have specialized lawyers to take care of customers from different religious backgrounds.

The e-Will service allows you to mention your digital and intellectual properties as well.

The whole process takes about two weeks to complete from the date of submission of the data to service provider. Once you have submitted all the information, the service provider sends you a rough draft to review. This is to ensure that interests of all concerned are covered without any ambiguities and reduces the scope for misunderstandings at a later stage. The customer must go through the wording carefully and make sure that it reflects his or her wishes as desired.

In case there are mistakes, even in the final copy, or you want to make changes at a later date, you'll simply have to upload and resend the document to the company with your corrections and they will draft a fresh copy. However, if you misplace the original draft, you'll have to re-fill the form and repeat the whole process again.

There are a few optional add-on services such as registration of the Will and appointment of an executor which help in implementing the Will smoothly.

Is it secure?

Both the companies have a track record of handling large-scale sensitive data and assure confidentiality. The e-Will writing process is just as secure as all online trading transactions. The information given by clients will be completely secure and encrypted in company data bases. Moreover, the companies also promise that the information submitted by the clients will be deleted immediately once the will is delivered to the client.

How much does it cost?

These e-Will services have been launched to promote the concept of making a Will online; one can always opt for the traditional way. If you get a Will made by a lawyer, however, you will incur a minimum cost of ₹15000 to ₹25000. This option is suitable for clients who require extremely complex legal assistance and would prefer a direct face-to-face interaction. Pricing for the same would vary based on the complexities that need to be addressed. An e-Will will cost you just ₹4000. Additional reviews are done at a nominal fee ₹250 per review.

❑

44

Trust

Estate planning through trusts will ensure that the estate passes to intended beneficiaries and minimize court proceedings in succession. It means by adopting a trust route, a person can avoid the issues which arise in a Will and make a ring-fenced structure to ensure that his future generations are well protected through a vehicle created by him and according to his directions.

A Trust involves transferring of one's estate to a Trustee for the benefit of certain beneficiaries which may include the person creating the Trust who is called the trustors /settlor/donors. A Trust provides for management of the estate during one's lifetime and also provides for distribution and management of one's wealth post demise in a planned manner over a period of time.

Traditionally, Wills have been the primary tool people use to distribute assets according to their wishes. But with families going to courts on disputes arising out of Wills either on the authenticity thereof, mental soundness of the person making the Will or alleged forgery, the Trust route created during the lifetime of the individual is emerging as a more viable solution to estate planning. The grounds on which a Will may be challenged are numerous, the time taken in India to get a probate of the Will in case the Will is contested could be several years and it could be a very expensive affair. Further the necessity to obtain a probate of the Wills in most of the cases entails the Will being made public and going to courts for obtaining a Probate. A public document, a Will is subject to scrutiny by anyone who wishes to know its contents. If someone feels they've been treated unfairly, they can contest the Will. Such challenges can tie up assets for months or even years, and cost your estate a huge amount of money.

In a Trust, a person transfers his property to another person i.e. the Trustee to hold it for the benefit of certain beneficiaries or it can be for the benefit of him. By adopting a Trust Route, a person can avoid the issues which arise in a Will and make a ring-fenced structure to ensure that the person's future generations are well protected through a vehicle created by him and according to his directions.

The Trust Has the Following Components

Author of the trust/ settlor- A person who settles the Trust or the author of the Trust.

- **Trustee:** The person who is appointed by the Settlor to administer the Trust and who accepts the responsibility of acting as a Trustee.
- **Beneficiary:** The person for whose benefit the Trust is created is called the Beneficiary.
- **Trust-Property or Trust money:** The subject matter of the trust is called the Trust property or trust money. Trust property can be in the form movable or immovable property viz. cash, jewelry, land, investment instruments etc.

For creating a Trust, legally there needs to be a

1. Certainty of an intention to create a Trust.
2. Certainty of the purpose of the Trust.

3. Certainty of the beneficiaries of the Trust i.e. the persons for the benefit of whom the Trust is created.
4. Certainty of Trust Property and transfer of the Trust Property to the trustee of the Trust.

Characteristics of Trust Structures Are As Follows

- Title to the Trust property gets transferred to the name of the Trustee.
- The Trust property constitutes a separate fund and is not a part of Trustee's own estate.
- The Trustee has the power and the duty, in respect of which he is accountable, to manage, employ or dispose of the Trust property in accordance with the terms of the trust and the special duties imposed upon him by law. There exists a fiduciary relationship between Trustee and the beneficiaries and thus the Trustee exercises a higher duty of care then a mere agent.
- The Trustee shall hold the ownership of Trust properties for the benefit of another or for the owner but never for the benefit of the owner alone. The owner who settles the Trust can be one of the beneficiaries.
- A Trustee's ownership is not an absolute ownership as known to law (i.e. trustee's ownership is the legal ownership not the beneficial ownership).

Types of Trusts

The Indian Law classifies trusts only on the basis of their purpose, namely private purpose (Private Trust) or public purpose (Public Trust) and religious/charitable (Religious/Charitable Trust). A Public Trust is for the benefit of the public and the beneficiaries are incapable of ascertainment and a private trust is created for benefit of certain specified individuals who are ascertained or are capable of being ascertained. Besides the classification on the basis of purpose of trusts, trusts can also be classified as either revocable or irrevocable in nature.

A trust created under a Will may be revoked at the pleasure of the person writing the Will or if the power to revoke is retained in the Trust by the Settlor. Further if the person creating the Trust retains control directly or indirectly over the income or the assets of the trust then also that trust would be deemed to be a revocable trust. A Trust which is not revocable is called as irrevocable.

Taxation of Revocable/ Irrevocable Trust-When a person looks at options of creating a revocable or an irrevocable Trust it is important to understand how income generated by these Trusts would be taxed. In case of a revocable Trust, the income of the Trust is taxed in the hands of the creator of the Trust i.e. the Settlor. The tax imposed would be at the rates applicable to the Settlor.

In case of an irrevocable Trust, the income of the Trust is taxed in the hands of the beneficiaries. The tax imposed would be at the rates applicable to the beneficiaries.

Trust Acts in India

The Indian Trust Act relates to Private Trusts and Trustees. Public Trust primarily mean trust created for either a public, religious or charitable purpose.

Estate Planning by a Trust Structure creating a private trust can be an efficient mode of planning one's Estate. Who should be a Trustee of your Trust? Traditionally people from the family or confidants are appointed as Trustees of their Trust by the creator of the trust. However, that entails appointment of two to three Trustees to take care of the trust in the eventuality of death or bankruptcy of the appointed Trustees.

Appointment of A Corporate Trustee Vis-à-vis Individual Trustees Has So Many Benefits Like

The main benefit is the continuity of administration, as a corporate will have perpetual succession as well as they have professional advice, as the Corporate Trustee can achieve efficient financial management of the Trust property by appointing experts for the same. Avoidance of changes in the trusteeship and cost of such changes with a large measure of security. They keep proper accounts of the Trust, audits of the same and review of the investments made by the Trust at regular intervals by competent persons familiar with business. They are impartial whilst dealing with the beneficiaries.

Protector/ Administrator of the Trust: While appointing a Corporate Trustee, a person creating a Trust may also appoint certain family persons as Administrators/ Protectors of the Trust settled by them to retain control indirectly over the Trust. By appointing Administrators/ Protectors the person creating the Trust can ensure that the activities of the Trust are conducted by the Trustee under the supervision and guidance of the Administrator/ Protector and as instructed by the person creating the Trust in the Trust deed.

Benefits of Estate Planning by Creation of Trust Structures

By adopting the Trust Structure for planning one's estate the following objectives can be achieved:

- Estate Protection because a Trust is a bankruptcy remote structure.
- Management of all types of assets through expert advisors.
- Accumulation of the Estate during the lifetime and post death through the hands of Trustees.
- Avoidance of family disputes leading to disintegration of family businesses.

- Retaining confidentiality, as obtaining a Probate is not necessary
- The person who creates the Trust can himself be one of the beneficiaries and enjoy the benefit of his own estate during his lifetime.
- Efficient Succession Planning by providing for children, grand children.
- Making provisions for religious or charitable purposes.
- Lower contest ability as compared to a will.

Causing efficient management of the Estate as a trust can be made operational during the lifetime and post death of the Client, providing for future administration of assets to protect against future incapacity and for incapable beneficiaries.

Conclusion

Though planning one's estate may feel uncomfortable, the cost of procrastination can be higher. Some people believe that estate planning will be a complicated, time consuming and costly affair. However, setting up an estate plan is not a complex process. In fact, it is quite simple and involves the following steps.

- You execute a Trust Deed where you appoint a Trustee, name your beneficiaries and specify how and when the properties of the Trust would be distributed to the beneficiaries.
- In a Trust, you transfer ownership of some or all of your assets (which can include investments, real estate, bank accounts etc.) and even personal property (jewelry, antiques or furniture) from your name to that of the Trust.
- Transfer of ownership of assets to the Trust can be done at any time after the creation of the Trust either by the Settlor or any other person.

- After you transfer the assets, you maintain the same access and control as you did before you put them in the trust in case of a revocable Trust.
- In case you create an irrevocable Trust then you can retain some control over the assets in the Trust by either having the Trustee consult you or by appointing an Administrator who will be consulted by the Trustee. You lose nothing, but gain the assurance that your wishes will be carried out if something happens to you, without the time or hassles of probate through the hands of competent and professional Trustees.

❑❑❑